THE WHITE FRAME HOUSE

The White Frame House

RAE SEDGWICK

DELACORTE PRESS/NEW YORK

Published by
Delacorte Press
1 Dag Hammarskjold Plaza
New York, New York 10017

Manufactured in the United States of America
First printing

Library of Congress Cataloging in Publication Data

Sedgwick, Rae.
The white frame house.

SUMMARY: A failed attempt at flying and the death of her
beloved grandfather, Paps, are key events in
a year of young B.J. Aiken's life.

I. Title.
PZ7.S4485WH   [Fic]   80–65838
ISBN 0–440–09018–0
ISBN 0–440–09019–9 (lib. bdg.)

In memory of my mother,
Helen Timmons Sedgwick Foster,
and her father,
Joseph Mallow Timmons

CHAPTER

1

The white frame house stood two stories high and was settled in the middle of a large and rambling yard. On either side of the house were flower gardens, filled in spring and summer with jonquils, tulips, rose bushes, purple and white lilac bushes, and two bird feeders. Maple and oak trees shaded the house in summer and protected it from wind in fall and winter.

B.J. Aiken was born and had lived her entire eight years in the white frame house. She lived there with her mother, Martha, her nineteen-year-old sister, Meg, her grandfather, Paps, and her dog, Dandelion. B.J. had a best friend, Press, who lived with her mother and father in a green house across a vacant lot from where B.J. lived.

The vacant lot was often the center of much activity —touch football, snowball fights, range wars. It also served as a short cut. More than once, had it not been for that short cut, B.J. would have been home late. She

1

was often so busy she lost track of time. Today was no exception.

B.J. raced across the vacant lot, her blond braids flying out behind her. She rounded the corner of the white frame house, jumped over her bicycle, which lay in her path, and stumbled noisily onto the front porch. Her book bag flew off her shoulder and landed with a thud squarely in the middle of the floor.

"Heck and darn," B.J. exclaimed as she got up and dusted herself off. She grabbed her book bag by the strap and dragged it through the screen door behind her. She hung her book bag on a hook in the hallway and squatted down to scratch her napping dog behind the ears.

"Dandelion, this is going to be the best party ever, you just wait and see," B.J. whispered to the sleepy dog. Dandelion thumped his tail on the floor and opened his eyes wide. B.J. patted him on the head, then half danced her way down the hallway and into the kitchen, where she found her mother and sister.

"I'm home," she sang out, taking an apple from a bowl in the middle of the kitchen table.

"Good," her mother said and smiled up at her over her glasses, which were smudged with flour and lard. She was rolling out pie dough.

"Oh, brother," Meg said from the kitchen sink, without turning around. "Just when I thought we were going to have a little peace and quiet."

B.J. ignored Meg's comment and flopped down in a

chair. She tilted the chair back on its back legs and glanced expectantly at the round-faced clock on the kitchen wall. Why did time move so slowly whenever she wanted it to go fast? B.J. forced herself to be calm by humming little tunes under her breath. Surely someone would ask why she was sitting around in the kitchen; then she would tell them about the party. But no one asked. Finally the suspense became unbearable. B.J. cleared her throat.

"Well," she said rather loudly, "I can hardly wait." B.J. waited for her mother or Meg to say something. Meg kept on washing the dishes. Her mother rolled out the last of the pie dough and placed it into a pie pan. Neither seemed to notice her.

"It's nearly time," B.J. said again and propped her feet on the corner of the chair in which her mother had sat down to peel apples. B.J., fairly bursting with excitement, folded her arms across her chest and tried to contain her feelings.

What if fifteen kids arrived at the front door and there wasn't a cupcake in sight? she thought. Why didn't I think of *that* earlier?

"Time for what?" her mother finally asked.

"For the birthday party," B.J. announced, letting the chair fall forward onto all four legs with a crash.

"B.J., you're going to break one of those chairs someday pulling a stunt like that!" her mother said.

"You should have told us earlier if you had to go to

a birthday party," Meg said sternly, without turning around.

"Worse yet, you could break your neck," Martha Aiken said.

B.J. stood up and put her hands on her hips. Her mother and Meg seemed so grumpy.

"Meg," B.J. said firmly, "this isn't just any birthday party, it's *my* birthday party."

"This is September," said her mother, placing a pie in the oven. "Your birthday isn't until April."

"Oh, Mother," B.J. said, dancing around. "They don't mind, really they don't. Anyway, it's nearly three o'clock and I told them to be here by three thirty." B.J. watched her mother, who seemed either confused or tired.

"Who doesn't mind?" Meg said sharply, turning from the sink. She held a soapy wooden spoon in her upraised hand and looked as though she wanted to pop B.J. on the rear with it.

"The kids in my class at school, that's who!" B.J. said with a big sigh.

"Now, B.J.," her mother scolded gently. "Don't be rude to your sister. She only asked you a question." She turned to face Meg. "And don't you two get into a squabble. I'm too tired to listen to it and Paps isn't feeling well today." B.J. watched her mother and Meg.

"And B.J., this is no time for jokes. Can't you see we're busy?"

"Mother," Meg said firmly, "I don't think she's kidding."

"Oh, of course she is," Martha answered. "Aren't you kidding?"

B.J. felt goose flesh pop out all over her body. Earlier the idea of a party had seemed so simple; now she wondered.

"I can tell by the look on her face that she's not kidding," Meg said. Meg glared at B.J. "How many did you say you invited?"

"Only fifteen," B.J. said in the biggest voice she could muster, which sounded like an itsy-bitsy voice instead. She stood and waited. There was nothing else to do at this point.

"You aren't kidding!" her mother gasped, slightly overcome.

"Oh, brother," Meg said, brandishing the wooden spoon. "I ought to thrash you with this."

"You really did invite *fifteen* people? For this afternoon?" Martha looked at B.J. with disbelieving eyes. She sat down in the chair beside the table. She put one hand over her mouth and shook her head. "This is just too much."

B.J.'s heart sank. "Oh, Mother," she said reassuringly, "they won't all come." She guessed there wasn't going to be a party after all.

"B.J., we do have other things to do in this world besides entertain you and your friends," Meg said furi-

ously. "And besides that, we're not made of money."
Meg turned to her mother. "I told you she meant it!"

"Now, Meg," Martha said. Martha didn't like to disappoint B.J. Suddenly she started to chuckle.

"This is not a laughing matter," Meg said sternly.

"Do you remember the time B.J. gave a surprise party for your welcome home from the hospital when you had your appendix out?" Martha laughed out loud. "I've never seen such a mess in my life." She stood up from the table and began stacking dirty pastry bowls.

B.J. watched her mother laugh until tears ran down her face.

"And were Paps and I frantic!"

B.J. suppressed a giggle. It really had been quite a party.

"Just like now," Meg said. She sounded angry.

"It could be worse," Martha said, rinsing the bowls at the sink. "Good thing I didn't put these away. I'd just have to get them out again to make cupcakes." She laughed again.

"Okay, you win this time," Meg said to B.J. "But you'd better believe that you're going to have to help."

Meg flipped B.J.'s rear end with the wooden spoon.

"Go find the balloons left over from the Fourth of July party."

B.J. hurried from the room before they could change their minds.

CHAPTER
2

B.J. found the balloons stuffed down in the bottom of a trunk in the hall closet. She sat down on the floor of the hall and began blowing them up. She could hear her mother calling out the kitchen window to her grandfather.

"Paps, oh Paps," Martha called, leaning out the back window. "Get the old hand crank and chip some ice off the block in the ice box. We're having a party." She called back to Meg, "Mix up some cupcake batter, would you?"

"A party? What kind of a party?" Paps growled over the sound of a motor.

"B.J.'s having a birthday party," Martha called out the window again.

Paps lay down his tools and shut off the generator. He struggled with the zipper of his coveralls.

"Paps, oh Paps," Martha called as she leaned out the

7

window. "Don't take time to clean up. The party's in half an hour and we're not even started yet."

Martha leaned back from the window. She could hear B.J. huffing and puffing on the balloons in the hallway. "How're you coming?" Martha called out. She wiped her hands on her apron as she walked down the hallway.

"Great, really great. Only three left to blow up," B.J. called breathlessly between puffs.

"Let me help," her mother said, sitting down on the floor beside her. B.J. handed her a red balloon.

"Meg's mad, isn't she?" B.J. asked.

"She'll get over it," her mother answered. B.J. watched as her mother puffed up a red balloon.

"I didn't do it to make her mad," B.J. said, tying a knot in a yellow balloon.

"No, I don't suppose you did. She doesn't always know what to do with you." Martha picked up the last balloon. "Shall I blow this up for you?"

"I thought I'd save it for Paps to blow up." B.J. took the balloon from her mother and put it in her pocket. "Thanks anyway."

"Paps is making ice cream. You know how he loves to make ice cream," Martha said, getting up from the floor. Just then the front screen door rattled.

"Oh, my gosh!" B.J. exclaimed, jumping up. "It's the kids, they're here!" B.J. jumped up and down and started gathering the balloons. She was dropping more than she was picking up.

8

"Coming! Coming!" she called out.

Dandelion barked and ran around in the balloons.

"You'd better let me hang them for you," said Meg, coming out of the kitchen to see what all the commotion was about.

"Paps usually does that," B.J. protested.

"B.J., Paps is too old to be climbing on chairs. He isn't getting any younger, you know," Meg said firmly and shoved B.J. in the direction of the door. "Go answer the door."

B.J. stumbled toward the door. Why was Meg so grumpy lately? Why had she taken to protecting Paps? What is the matter with this family anyway?

"Hey, B.J., let us in," someone called out. It sounded like Virgil. B.J. opened the door and was relieved to find, not fifteen, but five excited classmates dancing around on the front porch.

"Come on in, we're almost ready," B.J. said. Behind Virgil was Alice and Alice's little brother, Harold. B.J. held open the screen door as Lollie and Bradley, the Harris twins, brought up the rear. The small group bustled past B.J. They made a beeline for the dining table, chattering all the way. Where was Press?

"Hey, you guys, anybody seen Press?" B.J. called out as the group darted past her. B.J. craned her neck around the screen door to see if she could see Press coming up the walk. But no Press was in sight. Where could she be?

"B.J., come on."

"Isn't this terrific?" The gang was getting restless.

"We don't start this party without Press," B.J. yelled as she went out onto the front porch, letting the screen door slam behind her. She raced to the end of the walk, jumped on the gate, and waited.

"B.J., we're coming," Press finally called from across the vacant lot. B.J. watched Press's curls bouncing in the breeze as Press weaved her way through the tall weeds in the vacant lot. Press was seven and a class behind B.J., but that didn't matter to either girl. Press was shy where B.J. was bold, slow to act where B.J. was impulsive. As a team they balanced each other out. Or that's what Paps said anyway. Bouncing along behind Press was Put-Paws, a round, fluffy, orange cat. He was as constant to Press as Press was to B.J.

"I thought you'd never get here," B.J. said, jumping down from the gate and grabbing Press around the shoulders. Put-Paws dashed through a slot in the gate.

"Press, this is absolutely the best party ever. Homemade ice cream! Chocolate cupcakes!" B.J. looked at Press. "Where were you anyway?"

"I had to find Put-Paws," Press said quietly. "You see, he . . ." Before she had time to finish, B.J. leaped around in front of her.

"Do you remember those terrific balloons from the Fourth of July party? We've got them hanging all over the dining room. Right above the table." She waved her arm in the air to indicate the balloons.

10

Press stared at her. "Wasn't your mother mad?"

"Nah." B.J. put her arm around Press's shoulder. "You just got to know how to handle these things," she said confidently. B.J. grabbed Press by the arm and ran up onto the porch and through the screen door, which Paps was holding open.

"Your ice cream is going to melt," Paps said, laughing as the girls whizzed past him.

B.J. and Press dashed through the living room and into the dining room. The five guests sat around the oaken dining table, waiting for the party to start. In the middle of the table was a big plate of warm cupcakes. And Paps had given each guest a bowl with a giant scoop of ice cream. Meg and Martha had retreated to the kitchen.

"Okay," B.J. boomed, leaping onto a chair. Press sat down on the edge of the same chair. "We're ready to start."

"Yea, yea," rang the chorus of voices. Hand clapping filled the room.

B.J. picked up a spoon and rapped it against the side of the table. She flashed a big smile at Paps standing in the doorway between the dining room and kitchen.

"Attention, attention," B.J. yelled. "Who wants to sing 'Happy Birthday'?" Hands shot up all around the table.

"B.J., whose birthday? Who shall we sing to?" asked Alice.

B.J. thought for a moment and looked around. She studied Paps, who was in the doorway, casually lighting his pipe.

"I've got it! We'll sing 'Happy Birthday' to Paps. Yes, that's it! This party will be for Paps."

Paps looked astonished. He shook his head. B.J. beamed. She loved a good surprise and this was probably the best one yet. She waved her spoon in the air. "On three: One, two, THREE . . ."

"Happy birthday to you, happy birthday to you. Happy birthday, dear Paps. Happy birthday to you,"

sang out the small but energetic group. Harold's squeaky voice crackled above all the rest. B.J. directed the singing with up-and-down whooshes of the wooden spoon.

"Now, the goodies," B.J. declared when the singing was finished. B.J. leaped down from her chair, nearly dumping Press in the process.

"Press, you pass out the cupcakes," B.J. instructed excitedly. "I'm going to get a chair for Paps." The room began to hum like the inside of a hornets' nest.

B.J. ran to the doorway and dragged Paps by the shirt-sleeve into the room and up to the table. Paps resisted, but to no avail.

"B.J., you really shouldn't . . ." Paps protested.

"Sure we should. You're one of us." B.J. shoved Paps

into her chair. "Here, take my place." Press stacked three cupcakes in front of him.

"Happy birthday, Mr. Bush," Press said shyly. She smiled at Paps.

"But it's not my birthday," Paps protested, looking a little embarrassed.

"It is if we say it is," B.J. shouted, setting down a bowl heaped full of ice cream. "Right, gang?"

"Right, right."

"Pass the cupcakes," Virgil yelled.

"I wish our grandfather would play with us, don't you?" Lollie observed, turning to her brother, Bradley.

"I sure do," Bradley answered wistfully.

"I don't even have a grandfather," Harold muttered, looking at Paps.

"Three cheers for Mr. Bush!" Virgil shrieked, suddenly leaping out of his chair.

"Yeah, three cheers for Mr. Bush!" Lollie and Bradley sang out together.

"Hip . . . hip . . . hooray! Hip . . . hip . . . hooray! HIP . . . HIP . . . HOORAY!" Alice, Harold, Lollie, Bradley, Virgil, Press, and B.J. clamored at the top of their lungs.

"See, Paps, you really are one of us. Isn't that just grand?" B.J. put her arms around his neck and gave him a big squeeze. Paps was dearer to her than all the world.

"Better eat your ice cream before it's soup," Paps reminded her kindly.

13

"It's already soup," Press said, stirring her ice cream around. There was chocolate cupcake all over her face.

"It's still good, though," B.J. said, tipping up her bowl and drinking the rest of her ice cream.

Everybody ate seconds. Virgil even took thirds on the cupcakes. The clock in the hallway struck five o'clock.

"I've got to go," Alice said, jumping up out of her chair. "Harold and I have to be home for supper."

"Me, too," chimed in Virgil and the Harris twins. Nobody wanted to miss supper.

"Thanks a bunch for coming," B.J. said, following the group to the front door. She propped the screen open with her foot.

"Great party!"

"Best party yet."

"Cupcakes were the best part."

"I think the ice cream was the best."

She followed them to the end of the walk and watched them out of sight. Press was the last to leave. B.J. walked Press halfway across the vacant lot, then watched as she disappeared among the high weeds. B.J. hated to see the party end and her friends leave. It gave her a sudden feeling of being alone. She crammed her hands deep into her jeans pockets and found the last balloon that had been for Paps. She wondered about him. Was he really getting old like Meg said? A shiver ran up and down B.J.'s back. She broke into a run toward home.

CHAPTER
3

B.J. and Press were lying on their backs in the cemetery, under a freshly gathered pile of leaves. They had been discussing the September birthday party. Press's curly head and tennis shoes were barely visible as she lay covered from chin to ankle by a big pile of maple, oak, and hackberry leaves. B.J. was covered by the same pile of leaves, except that her hands and arms were folded across her chest. A chilly breeze played with the pile of leaves. Press and B.J. watched as it picked up a leaf and whirled it around the cemetery. Press broke the silence with a question that had been puzzling her for a while.

"B.J., why is this called a family plot?"

" 'Cause my family is buried here."

"Your family?" Press was confused.

"Well, my grandmother and my father. The rest will be buried when they die."

"I don't understand."

"Well, I don't either really. I just know my father's

15

and my grandmother's names are here." B.J. rolled over in the leaves. "See, this is my father's name." She pointed to the flat stone where she had been resting her head.

Press rolled over and watched B.J. trace the outline of letters carved in the stone.

"And that name is my grandmother's. These flat stones are called headstones." B.J. pointed to the stone where Press had been resting her head. Press watched intently.

"Well, she's not *really* there, is she? I mean, it's really just her name. Isn't it?" Press was talking rapidly.

"Press, don't be scared; it's all right." B.J. could sense that Press was frightened; her eyes were big as saucers. "I've been coming here for as long as I can remember and I'm not scared." B.J. rolled over and lay on her back, settling the leaves around her. Press studied the stone.

"Well, is she here or not? 'Cause if she is, well, I don't want to be."

"No, I don't think she's really here. It's sort of like a name card. Remember when we had to go to that big church dinner and everybody had a name card in front of their place?"

"I didn't go, remember? It was for Methodists, and I'm a Lutheran." Press felt snubbed just remembering the event.

"Well, I told you about it then."

"You brought me your name card." Press rolled over and lay down on her back. She rested her head in the pile of leaves, avoiding the flat stone with B.J.'s grand-mother's name on it.

"Well, these flat stones are like name cards. At least that's the way I figure it." B.J. folded her arms back of her head and watched a hawk soar overhead.

"How did your father die?" Press inched closer to B.J. All this talk about death was disturbing to her.

"I don't know for sure. He died before I was born; in the war I think." B.J. didn't understand war any better than she understood gravestones.

"It's kind of spooky here, isn't it?" Press snuggled up close to B.J.

"Sort of," B.J. answered. She watched the hawk make a lazy circle and drop suddenly to the ground. A high-pitched squeal broke the afternoon stillness.

"What in the world was that?" Press asked, sitting bolt upright.

"Hawk got a rabbit, I think," B.J. mumbled, obvi-ously concentrating on something else.

"Look, Press. Look over there!" B.J. said suddenly. She sat up and gestured excitedly toward a big maple tree.

"Now what?" Press felt weak all over. She looked nervously about; she had had about all she could stand of the cemetery.

"It's a flock of geese."

There above them, outlined against a brilliant October

sky, was the biggest flock of geese B.J. could remember ever having seen.

Press watched the V-shaped black ribbon weave its way across the sky. The geese filled the sky with loud honking. Press was relieved not to be talking about death. "If I could get up enough steam, I believe I could fly. Just like those geese. Don't you think so, Press?" B.J.'s face flushed and her heart beat wildly at the thought of flying—soaring this way and that, around the trees, in and out of clouds. B.J. was lost in thought.

"But, B.J.," Press protested, rustling around in the leaves, "you don't have wings." Press pondered for a moment. She thought she knew all there was to know about B.J. But maybe she was wrong. She asked cautiously, "You *don't* have wings, do you?"

"No, of course not. I would have showed you right off. I do have arms, though. The hair on my arms is like feathers on a bird's wing. I could just trap some air between the hairs on my arms, flap real hard, and presto. . . ." B.J. jumped up and began wildly flapping with her arms. In the process she scattered leaves all around, but mostly in Press's face and hair. Put-Paws and Dandelion, who had been napping under the pile of leaves, broke out from under the pile, spitting and barking. "I fly! I fly!" B.J. sang. She ran around the pile of leaves flapping and waving her arms. Dandelion yelped excitedly and Press's cat danced wildly about B.J.'s legs. Press sat spellbound and watched.

"You sure do raise a ruckus," boomed a deep voice nearby.

B.J. stopped flapping. Press jumped up from the ground and dashed behind B.J. Both girls were startled half out of their wits.

"Oh, Paps," B.J. laughed breathlessly. "You scared us half to death."

"More than half, almost total," Press said, coming out from behind B.J. Dandelion and Put-Paws circled Paps's legs excitedly.

"Didn't mean to scare anybody," Paps said. He bent over, patted the dog with one hand, and scratched the cat behind the ears with the other. "Your mother sent me to look for you. Said you'd either be buried up to your neck in leaves in the cemetery or digging around in junk at Morash's place."

"Paps," B.J. said firmly, "that's not *junk*; it's buried treasure."

"I suppose. Well, I figured it was too cold for—as you call it—digging for buried treasure, so I came here first." Paps sat down on a tree stump. "Whew, I'm winded." He removed his old felt hat and wiped the sweat from his forehead with a tobacco-stained handkerchief. "It's a longer walk than I remembered. Used to walk here often."

"Boy, am I glad to see you." Press ran over and patted Paps on the knee. She looked up at him with wide eyes. "This place is really spooky."

"Has B.J. been telling you tall tales again?" Paps coughed and blew his nose with his handkerchief.

"I did not tell any tall tales," B.J. protested. She jumped up on the stump behind Paps. "I was telling Press about flying." She flapped her arms up and down.

"And about name cards!" Press said, leaning on Paps's knee.

"Headstones," B.J. corrected. She pointed to where they had been resting their heads on the flat stones.

Paps looked where B.J. was pointing. "Oh, the family plot." He got up wearily from the stump and walked over to where the flat stones lay. He nudged one of the stones with the toe of his boot. His face suddenly took on a faraway look. When B.J. saw it, she got a funny feeling in the pit of her stomach, sort of like when the birthday party was over and everybody was gone. B.J. jumped down from the stump and ran over to where Paps stood staring down at her grandmother's headstone. She hugged him tightly.

"Come on, Paps, let's go home."

"Look, B.J.," Press called excitedly, and pointed up to the sky. "It's another herd of geese."

"Flock, Press, flock," Paps corrected gently, drawn out of his deep mood. "Cows are in herds, fish are in schools, and geese are in flocks."

"Come on, Paps, let's go home," B.J. begged, tugging at Paps's arm. She had a feeling that something awful was going to happen; more than anything, she wanted to be home.

"In a minute. Let me rest on that stump for just a minute longer." Paps heaved a sigh and walked over to the stump. Press and B.J. exchanged glances. What was wrong?

"Come on and sit beside me a spell," Paps said, and he motioned the two girls over to him. B.J. and Press sat down on the ground next to the stump. "It really is peaceful here, isn't it?"

A long silence followed, broken only by the honking of the geese as they passed overhead. B.J. watched as the V-shaped formation grew silvery and disappeared in the distance.

"Paps?" B.J. said, "if I try real hard, I could fly, couldn't I?" She leaned her head on her grandfather's knee. His coveralls were rough on her face. She liked the smell of machine oil and musty pipe tobacco.

"Well, I suppose so," Paps said thoughtfully. He laid his hand on B.J.'s head. "Yes, of course you could. You can do anything you set your mind to, as long as you believe you can. Believing you can is the most important part." Paps stroked B.J.'s hair. She felt suddenly confident.

"I guess we'd better get along home," Paps said finally, getting up slowly from the stump. Press and B.J. jumped up.

"Lean on us, Paps," B.J. said.

"Yeah, lean on us, Mr. Bush," Press echoed.

"No, I'm all right," Paps protested. "I've got my second wind."

"Let us help." B.J. took Paps's hand and placed it on her shoulder. Press took his other hand and held it in hers. "We can do anything we set our minds to," B.J. said firmly as she and Press led Paps down the road home. "And," she said aloud, "I will fly."

CHAPTER
4

B.J. spent every spare moment planning for her flight. She sorted through her mother's rag bag and made notes to herself in the little notebook she called her idea book. Evenings after school she practiced. Her preoccupation was evident to everyone, particularly Meg.

"I just can't tell you how peaceful this house has been the past few weeks," Meg said to her mother as she wiped the evening dishes. "Whatever it is, I'm suspicious. Whenever B.J. gets preoccupied, something is bound to happen. I wonder what it will be this time."

"Oh, I wouldn't worry about it if I were you," Martha replied. "Why don't you and Ted take in a movie tonight?"

Just then a crashing sound and a muffled thud rang out from overhead.

"What on earth was that?" Martha dried her hands on Meg's towel and started for the staircase. But before she had reached the landing, Meg passed her, taking the steps two at a time. Meg found B.J. lying under an overturned chair and two wastebaskets. Three volumes of the encyclopedia, one dictionary, and a piece of bulletin board lay scattered about the room. Meg cautiously lifted a pillowcase covering B.J.'s face.

"B.J.," she whispered, "are you all right?"

At that moment Martha reached the bedroom door. "Look at this room. What in the world is going on?"

B.J. moaned and moved slightly under the pile of debris. Meg lifted the wastecans gently from the top of the pile and turned the chair upright. She slid her arm gently under B.J.'s neck and pulled her to a sitting position. "Oh, Mother," Meg cried, "I'm afraid she's hurt." Meg lifted B.J.'s little body from the floor and carried her to her own bed. "And I've been so mean to her lately."

B.J. moaned long and low.

"B.J.," her mother said softly, bending over the bed and touching her forehead. B.J. opened her eyes and smiled at her mother.

"B.J., you creep!" Meg scolded. "You scared me half to death. I thought you were hurt. You big faker." Meg grabbed B.J. by the shoulders and gave her a mighty shake.

"Well, I could have been killed," B.J. shouted, rising up from Meg's bed. "I *will* be dead if you don't unhand me!"

"Well, you weren't. And it's cruel to pretend such a

thing." Meg made a grab for B.J. as she leaped from the bed to the middle of the floor. "Don't you ever pull a stunt like that again!" Meg shouted at the top of her voice.

B.J. stomped her foot and waved her arms. "You're not my mother and you're not telling me what to do."

"You're just a spoiled brat," Meg yelled. "And I don't have to take this from you."

"Oh, yeah? What are you going to do? Marry chicken-legs Teddy?"

"Mother," Meg wailed. "Are you going to let her talk to me like that?"

"All right, you two," Martha said. "I think that's about enough."

"Chicken-legs Ted, chicken-legs Ted," B.J. exclaimed, dancing about.

"Ted does not have chicken legs," Meg protested, drawing herself up to her full height. "And I'm not going to have you talking about him that way." She grabbed B.J. by the braid and gave it a yank.

"Ouch!" B.J. yelled, jumping up and down. Her brown eyes flashed. "Let go!"

"All right, that's enough!" Martha stepped in between the girls, separating them. Martha looked at B.J. "You don't seem hurt." She turned to Meg. "You should be ashamed of yourself. After all, you are the oldest."

"Me? What have I done?" Meg studied her mother's face. "Why do I always get the blame?" Meg reached for the pillowcase hanging around B.J.'s neck. "Isn't this one of our good pillowcases?"

"She's trying to choke me," B.J. protested loudly, making gagging sounds. She broke away and jumped around, dancing on one foot and then the other. "Anyway, these are my wings."

"Wings? That's a laugh." Meg made another grab for the pillowcase.

"How did this happen?" Martha asked quietly.

"I was trying to fly. When I took off, my tree limb broke and the whole tree collapsed," B.J. explained.

Meg looked around the room. "Tree limb? You'd better check her head for bumps, Mother. She must have hit it." Suddenly Meg gasped. "This? This!" she wailed. "It wasn't a tree branch, it was my coat rack! You used it to make a tree." Meg stared at the broken pieces of wood and overturned furniture scattered on the floor. "You ought to be spanked!" Meg lunged at B.J.

Martha stepped between Meg and B.J. "Meg," she said firmly, "I don't want to have to ask you again. I really can't take this bickering." Martha tried to pat Meg on the shoulder. "Please, Meg. Let me handle this."

Meg pulled away. "I'm sick and tired of her antics. She calls Teddy chicken-legs; she pours my Blue Midnight toilet water into the bathtub; she leaps around the room with our best pillowcase; she busted my coat rack, and it's plain to see that you're not going to punish her." Meg's face was red, and B.J. could see the veins standing out in her neck. "If Dad were alive, he'd make darn sure that she'd get punished." Meg stormed out of the room, slamming the door behind her. "And I'm putting a lock on my door," she yelled as she stomped down the stairs.

B.J. stood dead still in the middle of the room. She'd never seen Meg so angry. "It was only a dumb old coat rack. How will I even learn to fly if I don't practice?" She threw her arms wide over her head and brought them down with a slap on her thighs.

Martha sat down in a chair by the window. "Come here, B.J."

"Are you going to punish me?" B.J. folded her arms across her chest and tried to look indifferent.

"Should I?" Martha asked.

B.J. unfolded her arms and shuffled across the room. "I didn't really mean to break the coat rack." She looked down at the floor. "I really am sorry."

"What about those things you said to Meg?" Martha unpinned the pillowcase dangling around B.J.'s neck, picked a dustball out of B.J.'s long braided hair, and pulled her onto her lap.

"I'm too big to sit on your lap," B.J. protested weakly, though she secretly liked it.

"That will be the day," Martha said, folding her arms around B.J. The rocker creaked back and forth.

B.J. snuggled down into her mother's lap. "Well," she sighed, "I am sorry about the coat rack. I didn't mean to use the whole bottle of toilet water. It was an accident.

But Teddy does have chicken legs. Didn't you ever see all that fuzzy stuff on his legs? Looks just like a chicken to me." B.J. giggled to herself. She suddenly felt tired.

"Oh, B.J., you mustn't say things like that. You hurt Meg's feelings."

"I have feelings too, you know," B.J. muttered, raising her head.

"Hush now. Enough's enough. Be quiet and I'll sing you a song my mother used to sing to me."

B.J. could feel her mother's damp apron under her, could smell the aroma of cooking it gave off. Her own shallow breathing slowed and deepened with the rise and fall of her mother's breathing. She felt herself relaxing. Her own thoughts mixed with the tune of an Irish lullaby. Meg or no Meg, she was more determined than ever to fly.

CHAPTER
5

Early the following Saturday B.J. and Press were in the Aikens' backyard. B.J. was explaining to Press how the flight would take place.

"Now, what we have to do is get on top of Lucy Alden's chicken house. Then when I tell you, give me a shove right here." B.J. pointed to her backside. "Do we have everything?"

"I think so." Press picked up a sack and followed B.J. through the back hedge to the chicken house. "Aren't you going to wait for Alice and Harold?"

"They'll be here by the time we're ready," B.J. answered. She climbed up the side of the chicken house and onto the roof by boosting herself on a window ledge. B.J. turned to Press. "Come on, I'll give you a hand up."

Press handed B.J. the sack and then crawled cautiously up on the window ledge. B.J. grunted and groaned as she pulled Press up over the edge of the roof. "Boy, you're getting heavy."

"Am not!" Press gasped, struggling over the edge and standing up on the chicken house roof. The sun was shining brightly and October breezes chilled the air.

"Perfect day for flying!" B.J. sang out enthusiastically.

"Hey, you guys, wait for us!" Alice called, running into the Aikens' backyard. Harold came leaping along behind her.

"Alice, come on up," B.J. called, waving. Alice wormed her way through the hedge and climbed up onto the roof. Harold stayed behind and petted Dandelion. He was only five, not yet big enough to reach from the window ledge to the roof, for which B.J. and Press were grateful. Harold could be a real pest sometimes.

"Okay, we're just about ready." B.J. pinned her pigtails on top of her head. "Here, Alice, take this safety pin and pin the tea towel to my shirt. Press, you pin it on the other side." Press looked at B.J. curiously.

"Do what?" Press was having trouble getting the picture.

"Pin the tea towel to the side of my shirt and to my sleeve. I'll use it to catch the wind," B.J. said confidently. She emptied her pockets, squirming around as she did so.

"What are you doing?" asked Press.

"I don't want to weigh myself down."

"B.J., stand still!" Alice said, trying to pin the towel to B.J.'s shirt. She finally finished and helped Press finish her side.

"How do I look?" B.J. whirled around.

"You look like a bat," Press said with a smile.

"Bring me the frog flippers." Press dug into the pack and pulled them out. B.J. held on to Alice as Press assisted her into the flippers. Once in them, B.J. paraded around the roof. Her frog feet made a slapping sound as she walked. She felt very self-assured.

"Have we missed it?" yelled Lollie and Bradley Harris from next door.

"Nope!" B.J. called. She flapped the tea towels in the air.

"I guess we're about ready then," B.J. declared. "Press, you just get back there by the mark I made on the roof." B.J. motioned with her arm. "Alice, you'd better go down there with Harold and be sure no one gets on my landing strip." Alice scurried down. She looked relieved to be off the roof.

"B.J.," Alice called from the ground. "Is this where you're going to land?" She pointed to an old inner tube near the pear tree. B.J. nodded. Alice smiled smugly and turned to Harold. "See, I told you so."

"Okay, everyone—on three!" B.J. moved to the back of the shed, slapping the frog flippers on the roof as she walked. She could feel excitement building inside her. She turned around toward the front of the chicken shed and took a deep breath. A look of concentration came over her face. She signaled to Alice to begin the count.

"One," began Alice.

"Two," Harold and Lollie joined in. B.J. crouched low, ready to run. Press squatted near the edge of the roof.

"Three!" B.J. loped across the roof and, near the edge, raised her arms. Press gave a final shove, and B.J. was airborne.

"Off the roof, over the hedges, and onto the inner tube," B.J. sang to herself as she plunged through the air. She waved her arms and flailed her feet. She felt the rush of air in her face, could see the low-hanging pear tree branches looming up before her, and could hear Press cheering in the background.

The last thing B.J. noticed as she thudded to the ground was her mother's face with one hand over her mouth. I did it, she thought, I really flew! After she hit the ground, she felt herself slipping into a heavy dark tunnel of unconsciousness.

The next thing she heard was a deep, scratchy voice calling her name.

"B.J., can you hear me?" the voice asked, penetrating her foggy mind.

"Sure," B.J. mumbled. She started to raise her head. It felt heavy and thick. There was a dull ache right over her left eyebrow. "Oh," B.J. moaned and lay her head back down.

"B.J., open your eyes and tell me how many fingers I'm holding up." It was the same deep voice.

B.J. forced her heavy eyelids open; they were swollen

and sore. She wondered what in the world had happened to her. As her eyes came into focus, she could see three figures huddled around her. There was a strong smell of medicine. She recognized one of the figures as the town doctor. Try as she might, she could not hold her eyes open.

B.J. listened to the voices as they floated in and out of her mind. She tried to answer the doctor's question but the answer lay buried deep inside her head somewhere. Something cold touched her forehead. She forced her eyes open again. Her mother was holding an icepack to her forehead. The ice was soothing; it also helped her wake up.

"Where am I?" B.J. finally asked.

"Well, she's coming around." The doctor sounded pleased with himself. "It was a nasty crack on the head, but I think she'll make it."

"Mother," B.J. said, reaching out. Nothing seemed quite right; everything was fuzzy, and B.J. felt like she was floating.

"I'm right here, B.J. You're in Doc Chandler's office."

"She'll be all right, Martha," said the doctor. "Just take her home and keep her quiet for a couple of days. Those stitches can come out in a week to ten days."

"Stitches!" B.J. cried out. She put her hand cautiously on her forehead; there was a big bandage over one eyebrow. "Oh, no," she groaned. "I'm dying, I just know I'm dying."

33

"You are not dying. I'm taking you home and putting you to bed." B.J.'s mother sounded firm.

"Your head is going to be real sore and you might have a black eye or two. But you're not dying." The doctor stooped over and looked B.J. in the eyes. "And don't try jumping off Lucy Alden's chicken house anymore. You hear me?"

"I hear you," B.J. mumbled. She felt so sleepy.

"Do you have a way home?" B.J. heard the doctor ask her mother.

"Yes, one of the neighbors drove us over. She's waiting in the car outside."

"Let me carry B.J. to the car for you. She'll be wide awake by the time you get her home." The old doctor bent over and lifted B.J. gently off the cold metal table as if she were a fallen bird.

"I didn't jump, I flew," B.J. mumbled as the doctor put B.J. on her mother's lap and closed the car door behind them.

"Well, whatever you call it, don't do it again. I'll have to put a metal plate in your head next time." The old doctor leaned his head in the door and patted B.J.'s leg.

"She'll be just fine; don't you worry, Martha," B.J. heard the doctor say.

The engine of the old car started with a belch and the neighbor guided the car down the road. B.J. could just barely hear voices.

"Well, I'll say one thing for her. She sure covered a good distance. She nearly landed in the cinder pile."

"The cinder pile." It was the voice of her mother's friend, Edith. "My, my."

"The cinder pile," B.J. mumbled. She was impressed. "Did you see me, Momma?"

"No thanks to you. If Harold's shrieking hadn't brought me to the back porch, I don't think I would have seen it." Her mother held the ice bag on B.J.'s head. "You gave me a scare."

"Clear to the cinder pile!" B.J. smiled to herself as she fell asleep. In spite of her sore head and a few scrapes and scratches, she had a good feeling inside her. She had really flown!

When they arrived home, the front yard was filled with kids, bicycles, and wagons. The kids carried sticks and banners and were lined up in front of the Aikens' house. Bradley Harris was in the lead, with B.J.'s old battered wagon tied to the back of his bicycle. Alice was next in line with her bicycle, to which she had roped Harold's tricycle. Press carried a banner—a piece of white sheet tied to a stick. Lollie had her new red scooter, with her butterfly net taped to the handle. As the car rumbled to a stop, Dandelion barked excitedly and loud cheers came from those gathered.

B.J. raised her head slowly. She squinted her eyes and looked out the car window. "OH!" she gasped. "It's a parade!" She laid her head back on her mother's breast. "They're waiting for me." A wild cheer went up as Edith opened the door to let Martha and B.J. out. Martha sat holding B.J. for a moment.

"Mother, let me go. My friends are waiting." B.J. struggled to be free.

"Okay, but only for a minute. You have to rest. You've got quite a bump on your head." B.J. staggered over to her wagon, ice bag in hand, and hauled herself into it.

"One time around, then B.J. has to come into the house," instructed Martha.

"Sure thing, Mrs. Aiken," said Bradley Harris.

"You're a Hee-Ro, B.J., a real HEE-RO!" The small crowd gathered round the wagon. They stared down at the bandage. "Does it hurt bad?"

"Nope."

"Boy, did you really fly?"

"Sure she did, I saw it myself!"

"Wow! What was it like?"

The small parade moved ceremoniously off as B.J. described her flight in great detail. As the parade rounded the corner of the house, Martha laughed with relief; the wagon was now filled with B.J., Put-Paws, Dandelion, and Press. B.J. smiled and waved. Martha waved back. "Time to come in now," she said.

After B.J. went into the house and her friends were gone, Press sat for a long time in the wagon. Put-Paws snuggled down in a furry, orange ball between Press's crossed legs, and Dandelion stretched his stocky body out and rested his head on Press's shoe. They were not accustomed to giving up B.J. so early in the day.

Press climbed out of the wagon. Put-Paws jumped down and stretched lazily. Dandelion watched Press expectantly. Alice called to her from the vacant lot next door.

"Want to play hide-and-seek?"

Press considered for a moment. "No, I guess not." She didn't feel much like playing when her best friend was hurt. Press saw the shade go down in B.J.'s window and loneliness overcame her. She shoved her hands deep into her pockets and walked home, smiling to herself. "B.J.'s a real hero," she mused, "and I'm a hero's friend. I bet I'm the most loyal friend a hero ever had."

CHAPTER

6

Paps came by B.J.'s room that night. He was dressed in his jeans-coveralls and was chewing a wad of tobacco. B.J. heard him coming down the hall; she recognized the scraping sound his right boot made on the floor as he walked. He had been kicked by a horse many years before and had never fully recovered. He limped when he was tired or not feeling well. B.J. was glad to see his shaggy white head and bushy, bearded face.

"You asleep yet?"

"No. Come tuck me in."

"I'll only stay a minute. You've had quite a day. I'm sorry I missed it; the Wright brothers would have been proud of you. What a sight you must have made!" He paused and looked down at her. "You heard the call of the wild, didn't you?" Paps sat down cautiously on the side of the bed and laid his hand on B.J.'s arm. B.J. looked up through sleepy eyelids.

"What's the call of the wild?"

"Oh, it's . . . it's the call of free things to seek their freedom. It comes to all of us, but not many hear it."

"You mean like running away?" B.J. raised her head slightly. She had considered running away from time to time.

"No, not exactly. It doesn't mean running away so much as it does reaching out."

"Reaching out for what?"

"For better things. No, not better things, greater things. There's a difference. It means looking at the world with a new perspective, believing anything is possible."

"What's a spective?"

"Per-spective. It's the way we look at the world. Like standing looking out a window, with the shade down and the shade up. Or standing looking at Marlow's apple tree from his yard or from our yard; it just looks different. You get different ideas about things if you see them from different angles. When you were on top of the chicken shed, the world looked different to you. The house, the yard, the trees, didn't they look different to you?"

"Well, yeah. Things looked smaller. I felt bigger too."

"That's the idea. You were the same and the yard was the same, but you saw them from a different angle, a different perspective."

"You believe I flew, don't you?"

"Of course. Don't you?"

"Doc Chandler said it was only a jump."

"So who is Dr. Chandler? Does it matter what he calls it? You believe it, I believe it. Dr. Chandler doesn't hear the call of the wild. The world will always look the same to him. He only believes what he can see. The call of the wild isn't something you see with your eyes, it's something you feel deep within you. Try always to listen to the call. You've got a good loud one." Paps sighed heavily.

B.J. had a strange feeling in the pit of her stomach. "Paps, are you going to leave me?"

"Someday. But when I do, you must remember the times we've had together. No one will ever take them away from you. The times we've had together will always belong to us."

B.J. squirmed under the bedclothes. She felt a mixture of alarm and comfort. She held on to Paps's hand. "Paps, take me with you when you go. Don't leave me behind."

"I would never leave you if I didn't have to. I'll always take you whenever I can. If I leave before you do, I'll wait somewhere close." He tucked the covers close around her shoulders; she smelled his tobacco as he leaned over and kissed her forehead.

"Paps, how will I know where to find you?"

"You'll know, just as sure as you know the call of the wild. You'll hear me, just as you heard it. It's all hooked

41

together somehow. Go to sleep now. I'll sit beside you until you fall asleep."

B.J.'s breathing gradually slowed down and became more rhythmic. The last thing she saw before she fell asleep was the moon rising over the trees in the distance.

CHAPTER

B.J. recovered quickly. Over the days and weeks that followed, the wound over her left eyebrow shaped into a tiny hairline scar. The discussion she had had with Paps lingered in her mind. For several days after the talk, B.J. watched Paps closely. His limp seemed a little worse, and he sometimes complained of headaches. But then Paps seemed to be feeling better and B.J. thought about the discussion less and less. She remembered it only when she happened to rub her finger across the small scar on her forehead.

At Halloween Paps helped B.J. and Press carve two pumpkins into jack-o'-lanterns. One had a smiling face and the other had a monster-mean scowl and jagged teeth. They put candles inside and set them on the porch railing. When the candles were lighted, the jack-o'-lantern faces glowed and danced in the night.

B.J. and Press had worked on their Halloween costumes for days. When the big night came, B.J. dressed like a devil, complete with red horns and pitchfork. Press was a pirate, dressed all in black with a white skull-and-crossbones on her chest. They were so excited they almost forgot to take along paper sacks for their treats.

B.J. and Press stood on the Aikens' front porch, ready to go collect their "treats" or pull their "tricks."

"Now before we start, we have to make a deal," B.J. said.

"What kind of a deal?" Press asked.

"You don't scare me. I don't scare you. Deal?"

"Deal!"

They stole quietly off the porch and down the darkened street. Shadows danced about the trees and under the street lights.

"One other thing," B.J. whispered loudly as they passed under a dark and forbidding maple.

"Yeah, what's that?" Press followed close behind.

"Anybody scares either one of us and we stick together." B.J. turned around to face Press. The horns on her head made a shadow across Press's face. B.J. shivered and swallowed. "Deal?"

"Deal!" Press squinted her eyes and looked at B.J.'s red devil face. "I'm glad I know it's you," she giggled nervously.

"Yeah, me too." B.J. laughed, trying not to sound nervous. Both girls clutched their sacks under their arms and ran down the street.

They took turns ringing doorbells and yelling "trick or treat!" They soaped a few windows and turned over one lawn chair. Anything more serious would have gotten them both into "hot water," as Press's mother called it.

When they had their sacks filled, they decided to make one last stop, at Bradley and Lollie Harris's house. Every year on Halloween their father dressed up like a monster and turned their basement into a spook house complete with ghosts and crawly, slimy creatures.

"You scared?" Press looked at B.J. as the two of them stood outside the wide metal gate, which was swinging and banging in the breeze. Strange and mournful noises seeped out of the house and up to the gate where they stood.

"A little." B.J. knew that the noises were made by a record that Mr. Harris played. Still it was very convincing. "Are you?" B.J. asked as she pressed the button on the gate posts.

"Who-o-o's the-r-e?" a gravelly voice cracked out of an intercom. Both girls jumped.

"It's us," B.J. stood on tiptoe and yelled hoarsely into the metal box. "B.J. and Press."

Without a word from the metal box, the gate swung wide open. B.J. and Press moved slowly down the winding walk, which twisted its way around the house and toward the basement door in the back. Huge branches overhung the walk and tall grass grabbed at their legs. The strange noises from the house seemed to follow them. A cool wind played at the back of their necks.

In the dim light from the basement they could see a figure hunched beside the door. A voice called to them out of the night.

"Wel...come..."—the voice seemed to have fingers that reached out and touched them—"to Harris's spook house." The figure stepped out from the darkness and motioned to them.

"He doesn't have a head!" Press exclaimed in a hoarse whisper, gripping B.J. by the arm.

B.J. grabbed Press by the arm and darted past the figure. Sweat broke out all over her. Both girls scrambled ahead down the basement steps. "Let's hold hands," B.J. said breathlessly as they reached the bottom of the steps. B.J. could feel her heart racing. She was half-scared and half-excited about what lay ahead of them.

"B.J.," Press said, "maybe we shouldn't."

"Don't be silly. It's only pretend." B.J. held Press's hand. "Come on." Her legs felt like rubber as she parted the curtain before them and stepped inside.

They found themselves in a dimly lighted hallway filled with figures of ghosts and goblins hanging from long strings. B.J. and Press wove their way cautiously forward. Then something stringy and wet hit them in the face.

"Yuk."

"Eeek!"

Suddenly a body, all twisted and ugly, rolled out of nowhere into their path. The girls leaped over it, but just as they did, it moaned and tried to grab them by the legs. Both girls screamed. Next a mirror appeared in front of them. A bright light flashed and the face of a witch appeared. Both girls froze. "This is worse than I expected," B.J. whispered excitedly. Before Press had a chance to answer, the ceiling above them suddenly began to lower and the walls seemed to move in on them. B.J. and Press dropped to the floor and crawled under the shining mirror.

"And where do you think you're going?" a crackly voice rang out above them and on all sides. Arms and hands, some with fingers missing, lunged at them. Wet objects lay about the floor. Both girls were crawling ahead as fast as they could go, and their hearts were beating like scared rabbits.

"Faster, B.J., faster," Press cried.

"I'm crawling as fast as I can," B.J. yelled over her shoulder.

A loud train whistle roared out of the night, gaining on them from behind. Just when they thought they would surely be run over, B.J. and Press burst from the end of the hallway into a brightly lighted room. They flopped down to the floor on their stomachs. Their breathing was fast and labored, but they felt very brave.

"How about a glass of cider?"

47

B.J. and Press rolled over, glad to hear a friendly voice. There above them was the headless monster!

Both girls struggled to their feet, but it was too late—the monster grabbed them by the arms and held them tight. B.J. thought her heart would beat itself to death, it was racing so fast. Press felt faint.

"Don't throw them in the lion's den," a voice pleaded. "They're friends of mine." B.J. recognized Bradley's voice.

"If you say so," the monster said, and let go of their arms. Both girls fell back to the floor.

The monster retreated into a dark corner of the basement, and the girls breathed a sigh of relief.

Bradley stepped out of the shadows and squatted down beside them. "You all right?" he asked. "Sometimes Dad gets a little carried away with this thing."

"I'm okay. You all right, Press?" B.J. looked over at her. Her eyes were wide and she was breathing fast.

"I think so." She stood up and brushed herself off. "I don't want to do that again."

"You got anything to eat?" B.J. stood up beside Press.

"Fresh donuts and hot apple cider," Mrs. Harris said, walking up to them with a tray. B.J. and Press helped themselves.

"What were those slimy things?" Press asked.

"You know I can't tell," Bradley said. "Hey, thanks for coming. I've got to get back into the tunnel and help out." Bradley disappeared into the tunnel.

"You think he was the dead body on the floor?" B.J. asked Press as they finished their cider and donuts.

"How should I know?" Press replied. "I've got to get home." Press was tired of spooks and goblins. She wanted to be in her own house, safe and sound.

They thanked Mrs. Harris and went out the front door. Press seemed uneasy.

"What's the matter? Didn't you like the spook house?" B.J. asked as they headed down the darkened sidewalk.

"It was all right, I guess."

"Scared you, right?" B.J. giggled.

"Don't suppose it scared you any?"

"Who, me? Stuff like that doesn't scare me." B.J. was feeling very bold now that Halloween was nearly over. She pulled off her red devil mask.

"Got you!" a voice suddenly screamed out behind them. B.J. felt something cold on the back of her neck. She broke into a run.

"Hey, wait for me!" Press yelled, running down the sidewalk after her.

Footsteps rang out behind them.

B.J. ran all the way home and stopped when she reached the front porch. She fell into a lawn chair, huffing and panting. "What in the world was that?" she asked. She turned to ask Press. Press was not with her! "Oh, my gosh!" B.J. exclaimed, standing up.

Just then Press leaped onto the front porch, out of

breath. She stood facing B.J. "What's the big idea, leaving me like that?"

"I don't know," B.J. mumbled, shrugging her shoulders. She couldn't believe that she'd run off and left Press behind. "My legs just ran right out from under me."

"Fine friend you are." Press flopped down in a lawn chair. "I thought we had a deal," she continued breathlessly. "You stick up for me, I stick up for you."

"We *did* make a deal," B.J. said weakly. "I don't know what happened." She looked at Press.

"Scared, weren't you?" Press taunted.

B.J. folded her arms across her chest and gritted her teeth. She wasn't about to admit she was scared.

"Go ahead, admit it. You were scared." Press folded her arms across her chest and waited.

B.J. could see that Press was really angry that B.J. had run off and left her. B.J. felt a little ashamed. After all they did have a deal. "Oh, all right, already, so I was scared. What more do you want me to say?"

"That you're sorry you left me behind," Press said. Her bottom lip was trembling. B.J. was afraid that Press was going to cry.

"Okay, look. I'm sorry." B.J. sat down and put her arm around Press. "Come on, let's be friends. I'll give you my green agate."

"I want your blue one," Press said quietly.

"That's my best marble!" B.J. protested, taking her arm away.

"Okay, I'll take the green marble," Press said, giving in. She didn't want to push her luck. "And promise you'll never do it again."

"My green marble and I promise I won't ever do it again."

"Good," Press said, pleased with herself. "Let's go over to my house and eat our loot." Both girls looked in the direction of the vacant lot. "On second thought, let's stay at your place." They both jumped up and ran into the house. The screen door slammed behind them.

CHAPTER
8

The snow that began soon after Halloween kept up a steady pace throughout the winter months. At first B.J. was glad for the snow. School was often closed and she could spend entire days sitting beside the old gas stove, reading books or listening to Paps tell stories about when he was a boy.

Paps had good days and Paps had bad days. On his good days he worked in his little shop in the back of the house or sat in his easy chair by the fire. On his bad days he stayed in his room or slept in his chair. B.J. tried to be quiet on her grandfather's bad days; noise hurt his head. She didn't like those days at all.

During those long winter months B.J. even found herself missing Meg. Meg had taken a job in the city and would not be home until spring. She wrote letters often and wrote once to say that she and Ted were engaged. B.J. thought that would lead to great excitement, but it turned out to be no big deal, because right after that Teddy signed up to join the army. Meg's letters were sad after that.

One lazy winter day, when it seemed the sun would never shine again, B.J. and Press were wandering around the house like two caged animals. It was late February and the snowy gray days seemed to go on forever. It was too cold to go outside, even with tea towels tied across their mouths and noses.

"This is awful. I'd rather go to school," Press said, feeling bored. The school was closed because the roads were snowed under.

"Not me," B.J. said. "Something always turns up."

"Can Paps play?" Press asked.

"Not today; he's resting," B.J. said.

"He's always resting," Press complained.

"Not always. Just some days."

"Why?" Press propped her feet on the stove.

" 'Cause he needs to, I guess," B.J. said.

"Oh." Press didn't understand what was wrong with Paps. "Isn't there anything to do?" Press had just about decided that maybe she should have stayed home. But she didn't have any brothers and sisters, and it was lonely there.

"Let's go find something to do," B.J. said, unrolling herself from the blanket she had wrapped herself in moments earlier. The two girls went upstairs to B.J.'s room. They tiptoed past Paps's door.

"Shhh," B.J. whispered, putting her fingers to her lips. Press tiptoed along behind her.

"Who's out there?" Paps called as they slipped past his door. Both girls jumped.

"Oh, no!" Press hissed, clapping her hand over her mouth. "Are we going to get in trouble?" Her eyes were wide as saucers.

"I don't think so," B.J. said, meaning she hoped they wouldn't. She motioned for Press to follow her. "We might as well see how Paps is feeling. He's awake now." B.J. and Press tiptoed up to Paps's door and looked in.

Paps motioned for them to come in. "Come here." His voice was hoarse. "I was just getting up."

"No, Paps, don't get up," B. J. said, standing beside his bed. "Momma says you need your rest." B.J. looked at Paps. His heavy white hair was sticking up all over and there were bread crumbs on his beard. His eyes had black lines under them.

"Are you feeling better?" Press asked quietly. She stood beside the bed and hugged herself tightly. She was afraid Mrs. Aiken was going to be mad at them.

"Much better, Press," Paps said. "My headache seems to have gone away." He patted the bed covers beside him. "Why don't you sit down?"

The girls exchanged glances. B.J. shrugged her shoulders. "Are you sure it's all right?" she asked. She reached out with her hand and smoothed the old man's heavy white hair.

"Oh, come on," Paps insisted. Both girls eased themselves onto the wide double bed.

"You two look a little bored. Why aren't you outside playing?"

"Too cold!" Press said, scanning the room. It was dimly lighted and felt cold.

"Couldn't find anything to do," B.J. grumbled.

"I feel a little that way myself. How long have I been sleeping?" Paps rustled the covers.

"Seems like a long time to me," B.J. said.

"Want something to do?" Paps asked, running his hand through his hair. He was feeling better.

"Sure!" Press sat up.

"What do you have in mind?" B.J. asked skeptically. She didn't think Paps should be moving around much; she didn't want his headache to come back.

"Press, you open the curtains. But do it slowly because the light hurts my eyes. B.J., you bring me my robe."

"Oh, Paps, I don't think we should," B.J. said, filled with alarm. She didn't want anything to happen to Paps.

"Poppycock," Paps complained, throwing back the covers. B.J. and Press leaped off the bed. "I'm not finished yet." Press ran to open the curtain. To her surprise the sun was peeking through the gray sky. B.J. got her grandfather's bathrobe out of the closet.

Paps sat up on the side of the bed. "Whew," he said,

56

holding his head. "I'm a little dizzy. Must be those pills the doctor gave me." He put his feet on the floor.

"Let me help," B.J. said, kneeling in front of Paps. She took hold of one of his feet and shoved it into a slipper. Paps steadied himself by putting a hand on top of B.J.'s head.

"I can help too," Press said, squatting down to help put on the other slipper. Paps slid his foot in.

Both girls stood up and B.J. picked the robe up from the floor, where it had fallen. "Here, Paps," she said, holding the robe open. Press hung on to Paps to help steady him. She was trying not to look at his long underwear. She thought everyone slept in pajamas.

Paps worked his way into his robe with some effort. B.J. watched as beads of perspiration broke out on his face.

"Paps, maybe you should sit on the bed for a minute." B.J. tugged gently at his sleeve.

"I'm all right now. I want to show you something. Help me to the chair by the window." B.J. and Press each took one of Paps's hands and walked along beside him to his chair by the window. B.J. watched him carefully. Paps reached the chair and sat down hard. "There now," he said, drawing his robe around his knees. "Press, bring me my glasses. They're by the bed. B.J., bring me that box under the bed. The small brown one." B.J. and Press did as they were told.

Paps took his glasses out of their case and put them on.

He opened the box and took out something wrapped in a cloth. Both girls watched as he unwrapped the cloth, revealing a glass object.

"Here," Paps said to B.J. "Take this and set it on the window ledge, in the sunlight." He handed her the glass. "It's called a prism."

It was shaped like a ball except that it had hundreds of sharp ridges and bumps. B.J. set it on the window ledge, and when the sunlight hit it, it sent rainbows dancing all around the room. Both girls gasped with delight.

"Move it around," Paps instructed. As B.J. moved the prism around, the tiny rainbows moved too. She laughed out loud.

"Winter can't last forever now," B.J. said. "What did you say this was called?" she asked, bringing the glass object back to Paps.

"A prism. It belonged to your grandmother. I've been meaning to give it to you for some time now."

"To me!" B.J. said, holding it tightly. She looked at Press. "Isn't it grand?" Press nodded her head. She was overcome with all the excitement. "Can I really keep it?" B.J. looked at Paps.

"Of course," he said. B.J. noticed that his voice was hoarse. His eyes had a tired look in them.

"Come on, Press. Let's help Paps back to bed." Reluctantly Paps let himself be led back to his bed and tucked in.

"Can you stay for a while?" Paps asked as they tucked the covers in around his chin.

"Well, for a minute," B.J. said. The two girls crawled onto the bed beside Paps. B.J. took the prism out of her pocket, where she had tucked it for safekeeping. She moved it around in a piece of sunlight that came through the window and made a yellow ribbon across the bed. Everyone watched as rainbows played about the room.

Paps closed his eyes. Press grew sleepy and lay her head across his lap. B.J. played with the prism until she couldn't hold her eyes open any longer. She pulled a cover up from the foot of the bed and spread it over herself and Press. She fell asleep with one arm stretched across Press. The prism lay between them.

CHAPTER
9

Winter snow finally gave way to spring rains and sunny days. It was the time for flying kites, and B.J. and Press were busy building one, gluing paper to sticks. Put-Paws was chasing a ball of string this way and that, while Dandelion slept in the sunlight that streamed through the living room window. B.J. gave a whack at Put-Paws and just missed hitting Press's chin. Press yelped and fell backward on the floor.

"What's the big idea?" she demanded.

"Press, I'm sorry. Put-Paws is driving me nuts; can't you see that I'm occupied?" B.J. had just learned this new word and used it whenever she got a chance. Press looked up from her end of the kite.

"You're always occupied anymore." Press pulled the tail of the kite with a yank. "And why do I always get the tail end?" She waited for her answer.

"Well, the tail end is as good as the front end, isn't it?"

"I s'pose."

"I think there must be a rain comin'. Paps always says that when a rain is coming, the creatures get all stirred up. I'd say you're stirred up." B.J. continued gluing the kite.

"Are you calling me a *creature?*" Press looked at her in disbelief. She was about to pitch her end of the kite into the middle of the room when a loud boom resounded overhead. Both girls jumped. The room was suddenly dark.

"See, what'd I tell you?" B.J. went about picking up kite pieces. She was a little surprised at the fulfillment of her own prophecy.

Press was awestruck. Sometimes B.J. scared her with her knowledge of nature. "What was that?"

"Well," B.J. stood, drawing herself up to full height, "that," she began instructively, "was thunder, the herald of rain."

Press went to the window. The sky was dark. She pressed her nose to the window. "What did you say that was?"

"Thunder. Means a big storm's coming," B.J. commented matter-of-factly.

"Oh yeah?" Press was skeptical.

"*Herald* means to come before. Thunder before rain." She turned to look out the window at the rumbly sky. "Well, we can't fly our kites today anyway. Let's sit on the porch and watch the storm come up." A flash of light ripped across the sky, followed by crackly booms. Press looked nervously at B.J.

"I think it's already here. I'd better go home."

"In this?" B.J. challenged.

"Well, maybe you're right."

"I have an idea. You wait here and I'll be right back." She returned, dragging an old packing crate. Inside the crate were two blankets, a jar of milk, and a sack of cookies. Two yellow apples rolled around on the blankets.

"Where'd you get that thing?" Press pointed to the packing crate.

"Meg moved back home again."

"I'm sure glad she's your sister and not mine." Press wrinkled her nose. "What are we goin' to do with all this stuff anyway?"

"Come on, I'll show you," B.J. said enthusiastically. She shoved open the front door with her foot and backed out the door, dragging the crate behind her. Press pushed from the other end.

The door slammed behind them. They stood on the front porch and stared at the darkening sky. "Here, hold these things," B.J. said, bending over the crate. She handed Press the cookies, the milk, and the apples. She draped one blanket over Press's head. B.J. struggled as she turned the crate over on its end. "Okay, hand me the stuff and get in the box; I'll tuck you in." B.J. held out her hands. Press handed over the apples, milk, and cookies and crawled head first into the crate. She mumbled something inaudible.

"I can't hear you."

"I said, there isn't much room in here."

"To do what?"

"To turn around." Press was getting panicky. She backed out and started over. This time she backed in and settled cross-legged in one corner, smiling. B.J. handed her the food.

"Get ready, I'm coming in." B.J. scooted in beside Press, dragging the blanket around her shoulders. She struggled to get one side of the blanket out from under her and finally succeeded in getting enough to wrap around Press. B.J. pulled the blanket over their heads.

"Whew!"

"Snug as bugs in a rug. I'll have a cookie."

"Crumbs, you mean." Press dangled the sack of crumbled cookies in front of B.J. "At least they made it."

"Oh, well, we won't have to chew as much. Where's the other apple?" asked B.J., sorting through their supplies.

"I don't know. It was here a minute ago." Press sifted among the covers, looking for the lost apple. Just then a clap of thunder rumbled across the sky. Press jumped. "Whew, we got in here just in time." Press snuggled closer to B.J. It was warm and cozy inside the tiny wooden crate. "Tell me again about thunder."

"Well," B.J. began slowly, with a faraway look in her eyes. "You see, there is this big wooden bridge in the sky, and a potato wagon going over that bridge. Can't you just hear the potato wagon going over the bridge?"

"I thought you said it was thunder!" exclaimed Press.

"It is, I'm explaining it to you," B.J. continued. "There is this big wooden bridge, curved like this." She traced an imaginary bridge with her finger. "It has great wooden planks and a railing on either side. It's what the farmer uses to get across the creek on his way to market."

"With what?"

"Potatoes. He's driving a wagon loaded with potatoes, on the way to market. And the wagon has big metal wheels." B.J. tried to make a circle with her arms. Her elbows bumped the crate and Press's head.

"What keeps the potatoes from falling out?" Press interrupted, ignoring B.J.'s elbow on the side of her head.

"Sides. The wagon has sides on it." B.J. was slightly annoyed at the interruption.

"Oh!" Press seemed relieved.

"The wheels are big wide metal rims, and they make noise when they hit the boards. And that rumbling we call thunder." B.J. stopped, pleased with herself.

"Is that all?" Press asked. She was anxious for B.J. to continue.

"I could tell you about lightning."

"Okay." Press waited.

"Well," B.J. said, thinking hard, "see, there is a lamp

65

that hangs off one side of the wagon—the kind like your uncle has hanging in his barn." Press nodded in understanding. "The old man keeps the flame low so the light burns all the time; that's to see the way." B.J. was getting the idea now. "When he hits the worn spots in the metal rims against the wooden bridge, the wagon moves like this." B.J. rocked the crate back and forth.

"Hey!" Press said, hanging on to the crate. "Be careful."

B.J. smiled and went on with her story. "The potatoes bounce around and that makes the lamp swing back and forth. As it swings back and forth, it stirs up a little wind and the wind whips the flame around—making it burn brighter for a second or two."

Just then a slash of lightning ripped across the sky. Press huddled closer to B.J.

"See," B.J. said, pointing to the sky. "That's how the farmer sees his way to market." B.J. smiled. She had told the story just as Paps had told it to her.

A long silence followed.

"B.J.?"

"What?"

"How many times does the old man go over the bridge?"

"Until all the potatoes are to the market." They both grew quiet. The rain gradually stopped. As the two girls sat huddled under the cover, the sun suddenly broke through the clouds. A bright rainbow filled the sky. B.J. saw it first.

"Oh, Press. Look. A rainbow."

"It's just like the one your prism makes on the walls." Press suddenly turned to B.J. "B.J.," she said excitedly, "do you suppose there is a prism in the sky?"

B.J. turned to Press, somewhat surprised. "Press, what a great idea!" B.J. leaned out from the crate and strained her eyes toward the sky. "I bet you're right. Gosh, it must be a big one." B.J. leaned farther out of the crate.

Press took a deep breath. She was proud of herself. Just then the crate tipped over and both girls tumbled out onto the porch. "You had to go and lean too far, didn't you?" Press complained, picking herself up from the porch.

"Sorry," B.J. said, picking up the apples and rumpled covers. "Want an apple?" She held one out to Press.

Press took the apple and climbed up on the porch railing. B.J. climbed up beside her. She sat and pondered the rainbow, which was growing faint.

"Do you think there's a pot of gold at the end of the rainbow?" Press asked, breaking the stillness.

"I dunno," said B.J., watching the sun disappear behind a cloud. "Do you?"

Press shrugged her shoulders.

"I'll betcha one thing, though," B.J. said, turning to Press.

"What?"

"I'll just betcha you're right about that prism in the

sky." B.J. smiled and put her arm around Press's shoulders.

"You really think so?" Press asked.

"Yes, I really think so." B.J. smiled at Press.

Press smiled back, feeling good all over. If B.J. believed it, it must be true.

CHAPTER
10

The phone jangled noisily. B.J. jumped up to get it. "Hello-o-o," she sang into the phone. A long silence followed. Mrs. Aiken waited at the kitchen door for some word of exclamation, but none came. Finally B.J. slammed down the receiver and ran for the front door. "Be back," she yelled as she leaped off the front porch.

When B.J. returned, she was carrying a wooden matchbox. She found Press perched on the stone wall west of the house. "Oh, Press!" B.J. exclaimed as she came closer. "Wait till you see what I have." B.J. walked gingerly to the wall and set the box down. She stared up at Press. "*What* in the wide world do you have on your face? Are those Band-Aids?"

"How did you recognize me? I'm in disguise," answered Press.

"What?"

"I'm hiding from Harold." Press darted a glance

toward the vacant lot. Harold's new and very annoying game was spying on Press.

"Oh, brother. Is he trailing you again?"

"I can't lose him. He was in the swing when I got up this morning, even before I had my oatmeal. I snuck out the back, but just in case, I put this disguise on."

"Where is he now?"

"Over there." Press nodded her head in the direction of the vacant lot. B.J. could just see the top of Harold's head in the grass.

"Uh oh!" B.J. quietly picked up the matchbox and started for the house. "We'd better take this in the house. Come on." As Press jumped down from the wall, B.J. noticed that she was wearing red overshoes.

"It's part of the disguise."

"Oh, I see."

Press followed B.J. into the house. B.J. crouched down on the living room floor and set the matchbox down on the floor at her feet. "Now, be really still." She slid the box open. Lying inside were three tiny hairless mice, curled together in a ball, sleeping soundly. They were surrounded by wisps of cotton.

"Oh, my!" Press sighed admiringly. She leaned down and squinted her eyes. "Their eyes aren't even open." She squatted down beside the box. "Isn't it just too grand? Where did you get them?"

"Mrs. Walker, the school nurse. She was cleaning out her basement and she found the nest."

"Where is their mother?"

"No one knows. Look. Mrs. Walker even took the cotton out of her aspirin bottle to make them a nest."

"Out of her aspirin bottle?" Press whispered in amazement. Her mother would never give her the cotton from the aspirin bottle. "Her very own aspirin bottle?" Press thought for a moment. "B.J., are we mothers now?"

B.J. looked at the mice and looked at Press. "Well, sort of. I guess we'll have to be adopted mothers. Do you mind?"

"Oh, no. Do you?" Before B.J. could answer, her mother came into the room.

"What do you girls have there? What's all the mystery?" Martha leaned down over the box. "Oh!" Martha stood up and cleared her throat. "B.J., they're awfully small. They probably won't live."

B.J. jumped up from the floor in alarm. "Oh, Mother! Don't let them die!"

Press turned pale. "Oh, please, Mrs. Aiken." Press jumped up and tugged at Martha's apron.

"Oh, my. Well, we'll do the best we can," said Martha. "Let's see now. They will have to be fed and kept warm. You must . . ."

"How will we feed them?"

"With an eyedropper of warm milk and sugar water. And they must be kept warm, that's important. B.J., you'll have to keep them in your room. If Meg finds out,

71

she'll have a fit; she detests mice." Martha looked sternly at B.J.

"But they're babies," B.J. protested.

"Of course they're babies. But to Meg, a mouse is a mouse. She hates mice." She thought a moment. "Press, you'd better ask your mother if you can stay over, you two have quite a project ahead of you. B.J., there's an old alarm clock in the closet in my room. You can use it to wake yourselves up at feeding times. Get an extension cord and a light bulb. It's a good thing there's no school tomorrow. You may keep the mice, but they will be your responsibility."

Press threw herself at Martha, half leaping into her arms. "Thank you, thank you, thank you!"

B.J. leaned over her mice and sighed. "Hello, babies. Mother's going to feed you."

"Come on, girls. I'll show you where the eyedropper is and how to heat the milk. You can use the hotplate in your room if you're careful. The light bulb will keep them warm." Martha led the way to the kitchen cupboard.

B.J. and Press gathered everything together in B.J.'s room. The rest of the day went by quickly, what with heating, feeding, watching over, and fussing about. The names were the hardest. They finally settled on Billy, Tops, and Sam. They argued over "Sam" for quite a while, but B.J. won by letting Press feed the mice first.

By the next afternoon B.J. and Press felt a little ragged, but the mice slept contentedly in their little box, warmed by the twenty-five-watt light bulb, which burned night and day. B.J. looked out the bedroom window. "I think it's time we took them out for some sunshine." She was eager to show off their prizes. Press agreed. Both girls were a little tired of being cooped up in the small bedroom with an alarm clock, hotplate, three mice, a carton of milk, and a bottle of sugar water. The room was a little smelly.

They stole quietly down the stairs and out the front door, and found a warm spot on the stone wall near the house.

"I think we'd better move them to the front porch railing," remarked B.J. as the morning wore on. She had seen Monroe's cat sneaking around. "They'll be safer there."

"Sure." Press jumped down and B.J. handed her the mice. With the small box between them, they moved from the wall to the porch with the greatest of care.

"This business of being a mother is a lot of work," B.J. said as she set the box down.

Press looked up at her. "It sure takes a lot of time." She hopped on the railing beside the box. B.J. stared toward the vacant lot next door. She had squinted her eyes and put her hand up to her forehead to shade her eyes from the sun.

"What is it?" Press followed B.J.'s stare and squinted too. "I don't see anything," she said as she stared intently. "Uh! Uh, I do see something moving in the grass, down by the Aldens'." She followed the movement in the grass. "Do you think it's that stupid Harold trying to sneak up on us?" Both girls were annoyed at Harold's intrusion.

"Probably. He thinks he's a spy, but we can catch him. You go that way and I'll circle down behind him. When I sneak up behind him and yell, you throw that inner tube over his head." B.J. pointed to the inner tube lying by the pear tree. Together they sneaked from the porch, crouching low. Press kept close to the house, and B.J. picked her way through the weeds in the vacant lot. Cautiously they stalked their prey. B.J. could see that Press had made it to the tree and had the inner tube in her hand. She signaled to Press, who signaled back.

B.J. moved in close and could see Harold's cap just above the weeds in front of her. Just as she was about to let out a warwhoop, she heard a loud scream. Harold leaped wide-eyed from his hiding place as Press skillfully lassoed him with the inner tube. B.J. scrambled out of her hiding place and leaped square onto Harold, knocking him to the ground.

"Ah ha!" she announced. "We've got you!" She whirled him around. "You spy, you." Harold lay motionless, afraid to move. B.J. turned to Press. "Why did you scream like that? I was supposed to give you the warning."

"Scream? I didn't scream. I thought it was you. That's why I threw the inner tube." She stood staring at B.J. "I didn't think it sounded like you." She scratched her head. B.J. sat on Harold, deep in thought. Fear seized her. "Oh, no!" B.J. scrambled off Harold and ran for the front porch, yelling over her shoulder, "It was Meg, I'm sure of it."

They rounded the house just in time to see the final blow of the broom come crashing down on the matchbox. B.J. leaped over the railing and grabbed the broom. "No! No!" She struggled with Meg. "Why? They're only babies! They weren't hurting you!" she yelled. "Give me the broom!" Meg relinquished it. B.J. fell back against the railing and stumbled into Press.

The box lay on the porch floor, crumbled and broken. B.J. dropped the broom and knelt on the floor. She looked up at Meg with tears in her eyes. "They were our babies."

"Oh, good grief." Meg turned and stomped into the house. "They were dumb, dirty mice," she said as she paused in the doorway. She turned and ran into her mother.

"Meg, you shouldn't have, it will break their hearts." Martha stood at the doorway. B.J. carefully gathered bits and pieces of cardboard box and cotton. Press was sobbing silently, her head resting on her arms on the porch railing. Harold was standing just outside the railing, wide-eyed, with an inner tube around his neck.

CHAPTER
11

B.J. and Press leaned over what was left of the matchbox and its contents.

"I don't think I want to look," Press sniffed. "Did they know Meg killed them?"

"Ha," B.J. retorted angrily. "Are you kidding? They never knew what hit them." B.J. gathered up the dead mice off the floor. "We'd better go find an oatmeal box to put this in. Come on," B.J. grumbled. "We can't leave them like this."

B.J. fought back angry tears. She cleared her throat. "Mother, do you have an empty oatmeal box anywhere?"

"Well, there might be one in the trash." Martha leaned against the cabinet and watched B.J. pick the oatmeal box from the trash can.

"This will do. Come on, Press, we've got work to do." She turned toward her mother. "We are going to have a funeral." B.J. picked up the contents of the matchbox and slid it carefully into the oatmeal box.

"What are you going to do with that?" Press squinched up her face.

"We'll just have to dig a hole and bury them."

"Are we going to dig a big hole?" Press's eyes grew wide.

"I don't think so." B.J. picked up the box and headed for the basement.

"Are you going to bury them in the basement?" asked Press.

B.J. stopped and turned around. "I am going to the basement to get the shovel. Then I'm going to dig a hole under the lilac bush in the backyard. That seems like a good place. You can help me if you want." B.J. looked at Press, who did not speak. "You want to go find some flowers to put on top of the grave?"

"I guess so," Press answered reluctantly. She stood looking at B.J. B.J. waited. "B.J.," Press began, "I don't understand all of this."

B.J. looked at Press. "I don't either," B.J. answered. "But it's something we have to do. We can't just leave them like this, it wouldn't be right. If we don't think about it, it'll be easier." B.J. stood motionless, not wanting to go on but not wanting to stay either. Suddenly the oatmeal box seemed awfully heavy to her. She coughed. "You want to help me dig the hole?"

"It's dark in the basement."

"We're not going to dig the hole in the basement. You wait here and I'll get the shovel." B.J. set the oatmeal box down on the ground near the cellar door. Press moved back.

"Are you going to leave that there?" Press looked down at the box. She didn't want anything to do with the dead mice.

"You watch the box until I get back." A look of horror passed over Press's face. "I'll only be a minute." B.J. started down the stairs. Press hopped over the box and started down the stairs behind her.

"I've changed my mind, I'm coming with you."

"Press." B.J. turned around and bumped into Press. She could see that Press was scared. "Oh, all right, but wait a minute." She pushed past Press and picked up the box. "I'll set the box under the bush and it will be there when we want it."

When B.J. returned, having put the box under the lilac bush, she started down the dark cellar stairs. Press watched. "I'll wait here," Press stated matter-of-factly and sat down beside the cellar door on the ground. As B.J. rummaged around down in the cellar for the shovel, Press watched the box under the lilac bush. She did not hear Harold slip up behind her.

"What are you doing sitting there like that?"

Press leaped up, tripping over the cellar door. "Harold," she yelled hoarsely, "don't sneak up on me like that."

"I didn't do nothin'," Harold protested, stepping back slightly. At the sound of the commotion, B.J. hurled the shovel from the cellar and bounded out behind it.

"What's going on?"

"Nothin'. Harold is sneaking around again."

"Was not."

"Were too!"

"Harold, we're getting ready for a funeral." B.J. picked up the shovel and headed for the bush, talking over her shoulder as she walked. "For *our* mice." Harold hung his head and dug his toe into the ground.

"I'm sorry. Can't I come too?" Harold sniffed and wiped his nose on his sleeve.

"Oh, I guess so. But we have to hurry before it gets dark." B.J. began digging the hole.

"I have to go home for a second, I'll be right back." Press scrambled to her feet and was gone in a flash. Harold walked over and sat on the ground near where B.J. was digging. Neither spoke.

Press returned soon with a sweater. "I got cold." She blew her nose on a Kleenex that she pulled from her sweater pocket, and sat down next to the dirt pile.

B.J. finished digging the hole and looked around. "It's over there." Press pointed under the lilac bush with her finger. B.J. picked up the box and placed it carefully in the hole. With her hands she scooped dirt until the hole was full, then she patted the dirt down around it.

B.J. looked at the mound of brown spring dirt and felt a strangeness in her stomach, very much like the feeling she had had the night that Paps talked to her about the call of the wild. Changes were coming about that she didn't quite understand. Inside her she felt that old mixture of feelings, part sadness and part anger. Somehow things seemed so confused. A tear rolled silently down her cheek.

The back door slammed; B.J. turned to see Paps standing on the back stoop, his hands deep in his overall pockets, his familiar pipe in his mouth. She stood up and wiped her face.

"I'm sorry," she whispered to no one in particular. As she stirred the new grave with the toe of her shoe, she pushed back angry feelings toward Meg. B.J. turned around to find Alice holding a small bunch of dandelions. Press was huddled on the cellar door, toying with a button on her sweater. Harold sat motionless on the back step, just below Paps's boots.

"We'll need to sing a song and say a prayer," B.J. said in a husky voice. "Anybody know 'Roll, Jordan, Roll'?" No one did. "How about 'On the Other Side'?" No one knew that either. B.J. scratched her head. "How about 'God Bless America'?" she offered. B.J. was in the third grade, the most patriotic year in school. Press shook her head.

" 'Jesus Loves Me.' I know 'Jesus Loves Me,' " Harold offered. "Jesus loved the mice, didn't he?"

B.J. nodded and scanned the faces. All nodded in approval. "Okay, we'll do 'Jesus Loves Me,' " she said. Press got up carefully from the cellar door and walked over to where B.J. and Alice were standing, near the lilac bush. Harold stayed on the step. Only B.J. and Paps knew all the words, so Alice, Harold, and Press filled in where they could. After they finished, Press turned to B.J. "Who's going to pray?"

B.J. looked at Paps. "I guess I will." She lifted her arms wide. "Oh, Lord," she began loudly. Alice and Press watched her. She cleared her throat, glancing at Paps. He pointed to his ear. "Oh, Lord," she began again, "hear my prayer." She paused and then went on, "Lord, I don't know what to say, I hope you understand." She looked at Paps, who nodded in approval. "We did our best, I guess it wasn't good enough." B.J. could feel her throat getting tighter. Harold coughed; Press began to sniff. B.J. continued, "Please, God, take care of our mice, and forgive us our debts." She sighed. "Amen, Lord." Tears flowed freely.

"Amen," Press sniffed.

"Amen," Alice responded. She glared at her little brother.

"Amen," Harold responded obediently.

B.J. turned to look for Paps, but he had gone. She blew her nose and sniffed loudly. A cool evening breeze stirred in the trees, and the sun began to set.

Alice took Harold by the hand and started home.

Press pulled a Popsicle stick out of her pocket and stuck it in the dirt—on it were the names of the mice, scrawled in pencil. As she started home, she turned and waved at B.J., who waved back. B.J. watched until she was out of sight. She felt very much alone.

B.J. threw the shovel down the cellar stairs and went inside to her room. She slammed the door behind her. On her pillow she found a fresh daffodil and a robin's feather. She knew they were gifts from Paps. Everything seemed so confusing. She threw herself across her bed and cried.

CHAPTER 12

It was nearing the last day of school. Grass had begun to grow over the little grave and the death of the mice had been forgotten. B.J. was walking home, braids bouncing. Her gym shoes, marred and worn from a year of use, danced at her shoulder. Under her arm was a canvas bag full of a year's collection of pencils, erasers, pens, papers, candy, and old notes. Her favorite pen was an old Papermate, minus its refill. She and Virgil used it to pass notes back and forth in class. One would drop the pen and the other would pick it up. The pen would be laid carefully inside the desk until all suspicion was over. Then, when Mrs. Rockquist was not looking, the cap would be unscrewed and the note withdrawn. A response would be written and returned later, using the same procedure. Only once had the scheme come close to failing.

That fateful day Virgil dropped, or rather let the pen roll, from his desk top onto the floor. Unexpectedly Mrs.

Rockquist, all six feet of her, rose from her chair and began walking about the room, reading aloud from the daily reader. She turned down the aisle that divided B.J. from Virgil. On the floor between the two lay the fountain pen, nearly bursting with gossip scrawled on notes. Mrs. Rockquist halted quite close to Virgil's desk. She cleared her throat, looked up from her text, and peered over the top of her glasses around the room. B.J. heard Virgil whisper, "Up periscope, bombs away."

B.J. froze in her chair. In almost any situation Virgil could appear as innocent as a newborn babe. B.J. was never so lucky. As Mrs. Rockquist looked around her, each and every eye was intent on the text. Satisfied that all were attentive, Mrs. Rockquist started down the aisle again, reading aloud as she did. As she went, her toe struck the fallen pen and propelled it against the runner of the desk-seat belonging to Virgil. Now it was Virgil's turn to freeze in his chair.

Mrs. Rockquist stepped back. There, lying in full view, was the Papermate pen. She looked down at the pen for a moment, then looked at B.J., then at Virgil. Mrs. Rockquist stooped over, picked up the pen, and turned to Virgil. "Excuse me, is this your pen?"

"Oh yes, I must have dropped it." Virgil reached for the pen. He could feel the hair standing up on the back of his neck. Mrs. Rockquist laid the pen in his hand.

"Thank you," he sighed, trying not to look at B.J., who was sitting on her hand and staring straight ahead.

Mrs. Rockquist went on with her reading and soon returned to her desk. The pen passing slowed for two or three days, but never entirely stopped. B.J. shifted the canvas bag under her arms as she walked. Except for Paps being sick, it had been a good year. Ahead of her she saw Press sitting under a tree, her knees tucked up under her chin, her baton lying on the ground beside her. B.J. hurried up to Press and flopped down beside her. As she dropped her bag and tennis shoes, she saw that Press had been crying.

"Didn't you pass?" B.J. tried to hide her alarm. She was afraid of the answer and she looked around to see if anyone was listening.

"Yeah, I passed," Press whispered.

"Aren't you glad?" B.J. was confused. Why was Press crying?

"I don't think so," Press sniffed. She buried her face in her arms, which were drawn tight around her knees.

"Why not?" B.J. scratched her head and shifted position. It was clearly a serious matter.

"Oh, it's because, well, you see . . ." Press mumbled into her knees. She raised her head. "I'll never be a plum again," Press blurted out, sobbing.

B.J. watched her, baffled. "You what?"

"I'll never be a plum; I'll never get to play the recorder; and, *and* I'll never get to twirl my baton again, *ever*! Oh, oh, oh!" Press wailed and tears flowed freely.

B.J. could see that this was quite serious indeed.

"Listen, Press," she began, and then stopped. Press obviously wasn't in the mood. Together they sat under the oak tree until Press's sobbing changed to an occasional hiccup and sniffle.

When she began, Press spoke quietly. "Every day when I went to school, Miss Bakely would say, 'Good morning, my little plums, and how are my little plums this bright morning?' Oh, B.J., I just felt purple all over when she talked to me like that, and she was talking to me just like she talked to everybody else. I'd rather be a plum any day than to have to be a third-grader." Press pulled her knees up tight against her chest and rested her head on her arms.

B.J. was beginning to get an inkling of the situation. She leaned her head back against the tree and watched a hawk soaring in the sky. Suddenly she jumped up, breaking into song.

"When Sammy put the paper on the wall
He put the parlor paper in the hall
He papered up the stairs
He papered around the chairs
He even put the paper around Grandma's shawl."

As she sang, B.J. moved around the sidewalk with great flair. She glanced at Press, who was watching and sniffed only now and then. B.J. stopped in front of Press, squared her heels, and raised her hand to an imaginary flag and saluted:

"I pledge allegiance to the flag of the United States of America and to the Republic for which it stands." (*Stomp, stomp, stomp, stomp*—she began marching in place.) "One Nation, Under God. With LIBERTY, and JUSTICE FOR ALL!"

She snapped her arms to her side, reached up and removed her imaginary hat, and placed it over her heart. She looked toward the sky and sang triumphantly:

"God Bless America, Land that I love, stand beside her and guide her, through the night with a light from above. From the mountain, to the prairie, to the ocean, white with foam. GOD BLESS AMERICA, my home, sweet home. GOD BLESS AMERICA, MY HOME, SWEEEET HOME!"

B.J. threw her imaginary hat into the air with a whoop. She then tumbled down beside Press, now mesmerized. "That, Press Butler," B.J. exclaimed, a little out of breath, "that, is the third grade."

Suddenly Press could hardly wait.

CHAPTER
13

The first Sunday during summer vacation was always a big event. Everyone piled into the church pews in their best summer dresses and suits, smiling and nodding at one another as they did. The church would be filled to capacity—even the fathers attended. It was at this meeting that the congregation found out who its new minister would be.

The talk was that a new minister, a Reverend Hanway, had been assigned to their church. As far as B.J. could find out, he was middle-aged and would be arriving with a housekeeper. They would be living in the old stone house directly across from the church.

B.J. tied her braids on top of her head, and spit-polished her Sunday shoes. She was fastening her shoe-buckles when she heard the screen door slam. Grabbing her draw-string purse, which doubled as a marble bag during the week, she flew down the stairs, stopping at the landing on the way down to pull up her anklets and adjust her jumper suspender. From the landing she could see Meg and her mother already walking down the street. As B.J. ran to catch up, one braid slipped loose and fell down her back. By the time she caught up to them, Meg and Martha had reached the Millers' corner. Meg chatted on about Teddy, who was coming home on leave. At least Meg was in a better mood now that Teddy was coming home. The Millers' terrier, Max, suddenly bounded from the yard, barking and pawing the ground furiously. B.J. froze. Martha and Meg walked around Max and on down the street, leaving B.J. farther and farther behind. The dog turned on B.J., who had to make several attempts before sound came from her mouth.

"Mother," B.J. called out, trying to keep fear from her voice. At that, Max let loose with an extra fierce yapping and darted about. B.J. was afraid she was going to wet her pants. "Oh, Mother!" Meg and Martha, who had been totally absorbed in conversation, suddenly turned around.

"Hurry, B.J., we'll be late for church," Martha called. "Don't be afraid, Max isn't going to hurt you. He's only playing; he thinks he's scaring you."

"Well, he is," B.J. called, not taking her eyes off Max. Max saw that he had B.J. buffaloed and barked all the louder. Martha had almost reached B.J. "He's making me sweat in my socks; I'm sure I'm giving off those odors you told me about."

"What odors?"

"Those smells you said that a dog can smell when a person is afraid. Well, I'm afraid."

Martha glared at Max. "Lie down and shut up!" Max obediently slouched back to his yard. "Come on, B.J." Martha smoothed her daughter's hair. She put her arm around B.J. and together they walked past the dog. Max got up to sniff at them as they passed.

"See, see, I told you so," B.J. said excitedly. "He's smelling me. I'm emitting fears, he smells them."

"B.J., B.J., calm down."

BJ. looked at Max. "Go lie down!" she commanded, still with a note of fear in her voice. Max jumped up, barking wildly. B.J. looked up at her mother.

"Max, go on home," said Martha, and Max once again obediently returned to the yard.

"Why doesn't he do that for me?"

"Because you're not convinced that you can. Max knows that." By now B.J. and Martha had reached Meg. "Learn to be confident." Martha dropped her arm from B.J.'s shoulder and took her by the hand.

They arrived just as the organ had begun to play. B.J. slid down in the seat between her mother and sister, listening for the squeak that the hand pump made on the organ. She knew Virgil was in the back of the organ, pumping for all he was worth. B.J. surveyed the old church, its high ceilings and stained-glass windows. On one side of the church was a tall, narrow stained-glass window with Jesus knocking on a wooden door. It was one of B.J.'s favorites. The window faced the street, and she always made sure to look at it when she passed the church. She used to wave at the picture, but that was before Meg had explained that Jesus was knocking, not waving. On the other side of the church was a set of smaller windows, one with a dove, another with an olive branch, and the third with a cross. She hadn't figured this set out yet, but she was working on it.

B.J.'s eyes scanned the old church—she liked it here. She looked up at the platform and sure enough, there was the new minister. He was short and squat, with rosy cheeks and lively eyes. When he spoke, his words flowed, low and deep. B.J. thought for a moment and reached up to scratch her head. Meg jerked her arm down.

"Don't scratch in church," she hissed. B.J. frowned at her. On the next stand-up prayer, B.J. tried unsuccessfully to scoot behind her mother and get to the other side, away from the watchful eye and corrective hand of her older sister. But the prayer was too short. The prayer was followed by a sit-down song and then the collection. B.J. reached for her draw-string purse, reached her hand in, and pulled out a coin. She could hear the collection plate coming her way. When it reached her, she dropped in a fifty-cent piece and took out a quarter.

"What are you doing?" Meg whispered in horrified tones.

"I'm making change," B.J. replied matter-of-factly.

"You don't make change in church."

"Oh, yes I do!"

"Put it back."

"*Nope.*"

"*Put it back!*" commanded Meg.

"Can't." She passed the plate to Meg, who passed it back to her sternly. B.J. never flinched and dropped the coin down into her purse. She smiled at the usher, who was waiting at the end of the bench for the plate; Meg glowered at her and hurriedly snatched the plate and passed it on.

As soon as the service was over, Meg was after B.J., shaking her by the collar. Mrs. Aiken, who had stopped to chat for a moment, walked out the front door to find B.J. struggling on the church steps at the end of Meg's outstretched arms.

"Meg, what *are* you doing?" Martha separated the two.

"Mother," Meg protested, "B.J. took money from the offering plate."

"She did what!"

"I did not take any money, I made change," B.J. yelled.

"Oh, Mother," Meg wailed. "What will people think? I have been humiliated—a thief in my own family." Meg threw herself around dramatically on the steps and marched toward home, her head thrown high into the air.

B.J. and her mother stood facing one another. "B.J.,

you shouldn't have. You know as well as I do it's not right."

"Mother, it's all right. I had to."

"Why?"

"I'm going to take the new preacher for ice cream after church."

"On the money you took from the offering plate?" Martha was shocked.

"Oh, Mother," B.J. sighed, impatient at her mother's lack of understanding. "God understands, I'm feeding his sheep. I have to go, there he is." She turned and was gone in a flash. She yelled over her shoulder as she ran, "I'll be home for lunch." And she was gone. Martha looked helplessly skyward, then turned and hurried to catch up with Meg. She resolved to have a long serious talk with B.J.

B.J. waited outside the pastor's study for what seemed like hours. As the minutes dragged by, B.J. tapped her foot on the floor. Suddenly the door opened. B.J. jumped up and stuck her hand out.

"Hello. I'm B.J. Aiken. I've come to take you for ice cream." Reverend Hanway returned her handshake.

"Aren't you afraid it will spoil your dinner?" Reverend Hanway looked down at the tiny figure.

"Nothing spoils my dinner." B.J. flashed a big smile. "Anyway we'll walk it off on the way back up the hill." B.J. looked at him expectantly.

Reverend Hanway reached for his hat and suit jacket

hanging on the back of the door. "If you have to ask your mother, I could walk you over to your house and wait for you."

"Oh, that's all right. She doesn't mind."

Reverend Hanway buttoned his jacket. "Well, lead the way," he said. They marched single file down the hilly street, which led away from the church and toward the drug store with the fountain. B.J. saw Alice and Harold going into the drug store. "Hey, Alice, wait up," she yelled out.

Alice and Harold turned and waved when they saw B.J. B.J. and Reverend Hanway caught up to them. B.J. turned and grabbed the minister by the hand. "This is our new minister, Reverend Hanway."

"Hi," said Alice.

"Hi," said Harold.

"Hi." The minister grinned.

"You going for an ice cream?" Alice asked.

"Yeah, want to come?" B.J. swung her purse back and forth.

"Sure." The four of them marched single file into the drug store and up to the counter. Each climbed up on a stool and sat down.

"Vanilla."

"Vanilla."

"Vanilla."

"Chocolate." The three looked at the minister. He looked back. "I'll change that to vanilla."

B.J., Alice, and Harold walked the new minister home. He waved twice from the door and watched them as they waved back, then bounced up the street.

"You guys want to come for ice cream next Sunday?" B.J. asked.

"Sure," Alice said.

"Will Press come too?" Harold asked. B.J. was sure Harold was getting sweet on Press.

"Oh, I guess," B.J. said. "Everybody has to bring their own money though." And she thought to herself, I have to find a way to make some. The church plate is out!

"See you later," Alice said, taking Harold by the hand.

"Yeah, later," said B.J.

CHAPTER 14

Press knocked on the screen door and walked in before Mrs. Aiken had a chance to answer. They met in the living room, where Paps was lying on the daybed. Press walked over and stood next to the bed. Paps opened his eyes and smiled up at her. Neither spoke. Press reached out and laid her hand on his forehead—it felt warm and moist. She turned to Mrs. Aiken, who walked up behind her.

"Paps isn't feeling well, Press." Press nodded and followed Mrs. Aiken into the kitchen. "Want some milk?" She filled a glass and set it down in front of Press. "B.J. has gone to Clara's, she'll be back soon."

"Clara's?" Press reacted with surprise. Clara was the local beautician. "Why?" she asked, holding the glass of milk halfway to her mouth.

"She decided it was time to get her hair cut." Mrs. Aiken was beating the cake batter with a wooden spoon. "Want to grease the pans for me?" Press nodded and

Mrs. Aiken handed her the pans and the can of lard. Press got busy smearing the insides of the pans.

"Mrs. Aiken?"

"What is it, Press?"

"Is Paps very sick?" Press stopped greasing and looked at Mrs. Aiken.

Mrs. Aiken shut the cupboard door and stood for a moment. She cleared her throat and sighed. Without turning around, she said, "Yes, Press, I'm afraid he is." She squatted down and pulled out the cookie sheets. The screen door slammed. Press jumped from the stool.

"B.J.'s home," she called excitedly. She dashed into the dining room. Press skidded to a stop. There stood B.J. —bareheaded! "Oh, no!" Press gasped. "Your braids are gone!" A look of shock spread across her face. She circled B.J. slowly.

"Well, do you like it?" B.J. reached up and ran her hand over her short-cropped hair.

"Not very much."

"Why not?"

"You look naked!"

"Naked! I *do not!*" B.J. turned to look in the mirror that hung over the desk. "Do I?" She examined herself carefully. She turned to face Press, who by now had climbed up in a chair and was sitting cross-legged, her chin resting in her hands.

Mrs. Aiken came in and sat down. Press scrambled up on the arm of her chair. "Turn around, B.J., let's look at the new haircut." B.J. turned around slowly. "I think I like it. You look taller." She paused for a moment. "And older, a little more grown up."

"Well, I liked her braids," Press grumbled. Mrs. Aiken reached up and pulled Press from the arm of the chair onto her lap. She tickled her under the arms. Press giggled and squirmed.

"You'll get used to her without braids. She's the same old B.J. Isn't that right, B.J.?" Mrs. Aiken motioned to B.J. to come and sit in the chair with them. "The old rocking chair is getting too small for us, isn't it?" she said as B.J. slid down beside her. She began to rock gently.

The rocking chair faced the bay window overlooking the flower bed where the jonquils had just begun to bloom. The tulips were beginning to grow and would not be far behind. Two robins hopped about, cocking their heads.

"What are they doing?" asked Press sleepily. She snuggled her head next to Mrs. Aiken and looked across at B.J. She frowned slightly. She wasn't sure she would get used to B.J.'s hair.

"He's listening for worms," came the reply from Mrs. Aiken. Martha stroked B.J.'s head as she rocked. "The robins will be feeding their young very soon." As she rocked, she could hear their breathing getting slower and deeper. Soon the two were asleep. She sighed deeply, leaned her head back, and closed her eyes.

She awoke with a start. A strange silence had settled over the house. She listened for the sound of her father's breathing. She strained against the silence, but no sound came. She fought back her fear as B.J. stirred.

"Is it time to wake up?" B.J. rubbed her sleepy eyes and scratched her head. She was startled to discover her short hair. She looked across at Press, now batting her eyelids against the sunlight.

Mrs. Aiken coughed. "B.J., wake up now. I want you to run an errand for me." She stirred around in the chair and fought against her panic.

Press tumbled out with B.J. right behind her.

"B.J., bring me my purse."

B.J. went to the closet for the purse. She brought it back and handed it to her mother, who drew out some folding money and a piece of paper. She took a pencil and scribbled a list. "Here, run along and get these things for me while I finish the baking." B.J. crammed the money into her jeans pocket. She turned and started through the living room. "B.J., here. Go out the back door so you don't wake Paps." B.J. stopped, tiptoed over to Paps, and kissed him on the forehead. He seemed strangely quiet to her. She turned and tiptoed back through the dining room.

"Come on, Press, let's ride our bikes."

"B.J.," Press grunted sleepily. "You know I don't have a bike."

"I'll ride you," B.J. called behind her. "Come on." Press followed dutifully behind.

Martha sat for a moment, drawing her courage around her. She rose from the chair and walked slowly into the living room. She sat down beside her father, laid her hand on his chest, then on his arm, and finally on his forehead, all still warm to the touch. "Dad?" Paps did not respond. Martha laid her head on her father's chest and sobbed.

CHAPTER
15

B.J. and Press propped the grocery sack between them and started home. B.J. pedaled to the top of the hill and stopped. She got off the bike and helped Press to get down. She sat down on the ground beside the bike. She looked at Press. "Do you feel something funny?"

"I don't feel anything." Press thought something in the grocery bag had broken. "What do you mean funny?"

"I don't exactly know. Just a funny feeling." B.J. couldn't describe it. She stood looking at Press, who stared back at her. B.J. sat there for a moment, thinking to herself. Then she said, "Let's go home, I think something's wrong."

They got on the bike and were off in a flash, with B.J. pedaling furiously. What was usually a half hour trip seemed to be taking hours. As they approached the house, B.J.'s feelings got stronger. Fear seized her heart. Press hung on tight to the groceries with one hand, and to the bike seat with the other hand; the fender had begun to rub a sore spot on her leg. She did not notice B.J.'s changing mood.

They rounded the corner next to the house. A black car drove slowly away from the house. B.J. braked suddenly. "Oh, Press, it's Paps. I know it's Paps." B.J. jumped off her bike, letting Press and the groceries spill to the ground. She ran the rest of the way home and burst through the front door. The daybed was empty. Her mother was sitting in the chair looking out the bay window.

"Where is he?" B.J. demanded. She stared at the daybed. "Where is he?" she yelled. She spun around and faced her mother. "You knew he was leaving. You knew and you didn't tell me. You sent me off to the dumb grocery store!" She clenched her fists and waved them in the air, bringing them down hard at her sides. "You made me miss his going," she shouted. "How could you do this to me?" She stood helpless. "He told me I could go along; he said he'd never leave me. How will I ever find him?" B.J. was nearly screaming.

"B.J., come here." Her mother held out her arms.

"No, I won't! Don't ever talk to me, *ever!*" Martha reached out for her. "Don't touch me!" B.J. shouted. She recoiled and ran from the house.

CHAPTER
16

B.J. climbed the old wooden ladder to the tree house. The sun was going down; the air was cool. An old rug was folded up in the corner of the tree house, and she wrapped herself up in it. The sky was barely visible through the top of the tree house. B.J. pulled the rug tightly around her and watched the clouds as they floated silently overhead.

That strange heaviness swept over her again, but she knew that Paps would not come to explain it away this time. "I am alone," she whispered to herself. She felt afraid—of what, she did not know. Through a crack in the tree house wall she could see the yard below. Huddled silently in the corner of the tree house, B.J. wanted comfort but did not know where to find it.

Birds sang, squirrels chattered. The world did not seem to change much or take notice of the turn her life had taken. B.J. stirred around in the tree house. Through the crack she could see that activity had begun in the house.

The minister was just leaving. "Turncoat," she muttered, and vowed not to buy him any more ice cream. People came and went all afternoon. B.J. stayed in the tree house.

Toward evening a voice called to her. She refused to answer. "B.J.?" the voice called out again. It was Press. A rock hit the side of the tree house. B.J. craned her neck outside.

B.J. called to her, "Go away!"

"Come down."

"Can't."

"Why?"

"Because, that's why."

"Oh." Silence followed. B.J. looked down again at the ground. Press was gone. B.J. ducked back inside and wrapped herself up in the rug.

"B.J., B.J.," Press called a bit later. B.J. did not answer. In the silence that followed, B.J. felt confused and lonely. When she heard a stirring at the foot of the tree, she unwrapped herself from the rug, crawled to the doorway, and looked down. Press was at the foot of the tree, unrolling her sleeping bag.

Press scooted inside the bag and pulled her big stuffed bear in after her. B.J. watched her for a moment, then went back into the tree house. Wrapped up in her rug, she fell asleep crying.

Suddenly she opened her eyes. Something had stirred in the darkness beside her. "Who's there?" she cried, reaching out into the night.

"It's me!" Press said. "I got scared down there by myself. Let me stay."

"Oh, all right." B.J. hoped Press couldn't see her crying. Somehow the dark was less empty with Press there. There was room for both in the rug, and they soon fell fast asleep. The stuffed bear lay across the doorway.

B.J. awoke early the next day. She watched the sun rise, bright red with golden edges.

Press stirred, then stretched and yawned. She looked at B.J. "I'm hungry," she announced. The girls got up. B.J. tossed the rug to one side and started down the ladder. "You coming?" she asked Press.

"I don't know how, I never was up here before," Press said worriedly.

"How did you get up?"

"I don't know, it was dark and I was scared, that's all." Press looked over the edge. Boards were nailed every which way all down the trunk.

"You come right on down like this. I'll go first." B.J. went on down the tree trunk one board at a time; Press followed behind.

When they were on the ground, Press remembered her bear. "Herkel's still up there."

B.J. looked at her and sighed. She climbed back up and brought down the bear. "Here is your dumb bear."

"Thanks." Press tucked the bear under her arm and turned to go home.

"Where you going?"

"Home." Press turned toward B.J. "Oh, I guess I'm not going anywhere." She followed B.J. up to the house. "I do have to go to the bathroom."

"Okay." They went in the back door quietly. Everyone was still asleep. In the living room the daybed was empty. The room was filled with flowers. B.J. closed the sliding doors quietly and turned to Press.

"Press, Paps is *gone*," B.J. whispered. She felt numb all over.

"Gone!" Press said with alarm. "What do you mean, gone?" Something was very wrong. "Where did he go, B.J.?"

"He's dead!" B.J. fought back angry tears.

"Dead? Does that mean we'll never see him again?" Press couldn't believe that Paps was really gone.

"I guess so." B.J. felt empty. She slid down to the hallway floor. Press sat down, and both girls were silent for a long time. B.J. pulled her knees up to her and wrapped her arms around them. She buried her face in her arms. Silence filled the air.

"B.J., what is dead anyway?" Press was confused. She had just seen Paps yesterday. How could it be that she and B.J. would never see him again?

"I don't know for sure, Press," B.J. mumbled without looking up. "I really don't know." She felt more alone than ever, even with Press right next to her.

CHAPTER 17

B.J. heard a voice call to her. She looked up from where she was still sitting on the hall floor. Press was gone. Meg was standing over her.

"What do you want?" B.J. said, blinking her eyes against the light.

"Just to be with you, I guess." She sat down beside B.J. B.J. could see that she had been crying.

B.J. felt strange there with Meg—usually they fought. B.J. didn't know what to say. After what seemed like a long time, Meg spoke.

"I know this is hard for you." Meg's voice was hoarse.

"How do you know that?" B.J. wondered how Meg could possibly know how she was feeling.

"Because it's hard for me," Meg said quietly. She sighed and twisted the handkerchief she was holding. B.J. swallowed hard. "I was about your age when our father died," Meg added.

It suddenly occurred to B.J. that Meg must have loved

their father as much as she loved Paps. She looked up at her sister, who had begun to cry. B.J. reached over and touched her hand.

"I'm sorry, Meg, really I am." B.J. could hold back her own tears no longer. Meg put her arms around B.J.

"Me too, B.J., me too," Meg said, sobbing. Meg rocked them gently back and forth. B.J. lay quietly against her.

"What's going to happen next?" she finally asked.

Meg cleared her throat. "People will come and go. There will be a lot of flowers," she began.

"No, I mean . . ." B.J. interrupted. Suddenly she coudn't bring herself to finish the sentence.

"Oh, you mean with Paps," Meg said. She sighed deeply.

B.J. nodded her head. She wanted to know, and at the same time she didn't. Her stomach was tying itself in little knots.

Meg didn't know exactly how to start.

"Where is Paps anyway?" B.J. asked.

"His body is at the funeral home, but his soul is in heaven with God." Meg paused and blew her nose.

"Are we going to see him?"

"You can't see a soul, B.J. The soul is something invisible."

"I mean his body, Meg. Are we going to see his body?"

"I don't know if you should, B.J."

"Why not? I want to see Paps." B.J. gripped Meg's arm. "Take me to see him, will you?"

"B.J., it wouldn't really be Paps. You understand that, don't you?"

"Take me to see him now," B.J. said, standing up. Meg stayed on the floor.

"I have to talk to Mother," Meg said, getting up. "We weren't going to take you to the funeral."

"What do you mean, you weren't going to take me to the funeral?" B.J. couldn't believe her ears.

"We didn't think it would be good for you. You're sort of . . ."

"Sort of what, Meg? Sort of what?" B.J. was shouting. Her face grew hot.

"High strung," Meg said. "We thought maybe it would upset you too much."

"Upset me!" B.J. yelled. "Upset me!" B.J. stamped her foot. "How could you not take me to see Paps?"

"All right, all right. Be quiet. You're going to upset Mother. I'll take you. But believe me, you're not going to like it. Paps is going to be laid out in a casket in his best suit. He's going to look like he's sleeping, but he isn't. People will try to look brave and happy, but they won't be. After the funeral the casket will be taken to the cemetery and put in the ground. Just like my father and my grandmother. And believe me," now Meg was shouting, "you're not going to like it one bit." Meg stomped up the stairs and slammed her bedroom door.

B.J. ran upstairs to change her clothes. She was going to the funeral and nobody was going to stop her.

Later that day B.J. went with Meg and her mother to the funeral home. It was a large gray building downtown that B.J. had never been in before. Many people that B.J. knew were there. She looked about the room. Meg was right. In the front of the room was the large brown box Meg had called a casket, and surrounding it were flowers, tons of flowers. Soft music filled the room. A heavy, sweet odor hung in the air.

B.J. sat with her family in a corner, separated from the other part of the room by a heavy brown curtain. The funeral began quietly. She watched as the minister went to the front of the room and prayed. There was more music, and then people began to line up in front of the casket. Some were crying and others were trying to smile. Meg was right: B.J. didn't like this at all. No one seemed to be themselves. B.J. felt a funny gnawing in the pit of her stomach. Finally their turn came to walk past the casket. Meg and Mother went first. Someone put a stool on the floor for B.J. to stand on.

B.J. climbed up on the stool and looked in the box. "Paps," she whispered. She reached over and touched his face. It was cold and greasy. Meg was right! Paps looked like he was sleeping, but he wasn't. Nothing was making any sense. B.J. wanted Paps to speak to her. She wanted him to tell her everything was all right. But he didn't move. B.J. climbed down off the stool and followed her mother and Meg to a big, shiny black car waiting outside. There was a whirring inside her head.

The long black car bore them away, Mother, Meg, and B.J., followed by a line of other cars, moving slowly. Within a short time they came to the cemetery that B.J. knew so well. B.J. looked out the car window and saw a great pile of dirt beside a large hole. An open tent sheltered the hole and the mound of dirt. The brown box was in the back of the car in front of her.

All at once she remembered the oatmeal box and the hole under the lilac bush. It was all becoming clearer.

Meg helped Martha out of the car and up toward the tent. B.J. followed, her mind whirring. She barely noticed what was happening.

As she watched the casket being lowered into the ground, she knew. Paps was not coming back; he was not taking her with him. He probably wasn't even waiting on the other side. Anger swelled up within B.J., more intense than she had ever known. She watched as a man threw dirt in on top of the box. This is "dead," she said to herself, and I don't like it! B.J. kicked in a piece of dirt with the toe of her shoe, watched it tumble down and break against the box. Somewhere within her, she felt a door close.

CHAPTER 18

B.J. lay on her back, her arms under her head. She gazed up as a spider spun its web on the ceiling above. It dropped down a ways by an invisible cord and then climbed slowly back to its web by the same invisible string. The morning sun shone brightly through the window, bouncing off the dresser mirror. B.J. watched as little flecks of dust drifted up and down.

The chatter of a squirrel in the tree outside her window mingled with the call of the redbird and the rat-a-tat-tat of the downy woodpecker. All the familiar sights and sounds were the same, but B.J. didn't feel the same when she heard them; the events of the last days had confused her.

She sat upright and swung her legs over the side of her bed. Across the room, on top of the trunk, was the small wooden box in which she stored her treasures. She went and picked up the box, and returned with it to the bed. She set the box down carefully and flipped back the lid. Her fingers stirred among the contents, revealing a butterfly wing, a walnut shell, a twig, a seashell, three marbles, a pen. . . . She stopped when she found the small prism that Paps had given her.

B.J. lay down on the floor where the sunlight fell and held the prism up toward the window. She played beams this way and that, bringing them to rest below the spider web near the ceiling. Rainbows danced around on the yellow ceiling, reminding B.J. of the colors in the woods down by the creek, where Paps had taken her tadpoling.

She thought of the tadpole days and other days she and Paps had spent there, walking and talking in the woods, then filled with grapevines, dog-toothed violets, jack-in-the-pulpits, and bright sunlight. She and Paps had chosen a grapevine for their swing and returned there often on hot summer days to cool off and swing on the vine, which grew beside the creek. She felt a tugging deep within her.

B.J. lay there on the floor for some time, twisting and turning the prism in the sunlight, watching the rainbows play about the room. When a rainbow fell across the sailor hat on her shelf, she remembered the time Paps had given it to her.

It had been a cool spring day, "sweater weather," Paps called it. She and Paps were on their afternoon stroll, he with his cane and she with an improvised walking stick. Paps wore his jacket and his rumpled felt hat, B.J.

wore a sweater and was bareheaded. The sky was a crystal blue, with an occasional fleecy cloud. There was not a hint of rain in the air. They had walked for several blocks in silence. Suddenly, out of a clear sky, warm drops of water fell on them. B.J. looked up at Paps. There were no clouds in the sky; Paps reached inside his coat and pulled out the old sailor hat. "Thought you might need this." He set the hat down on her head. The warm spring rain lasted for only a few minutes. When they reached the corner, B.J. could see that it hadn't rained there.

"Why did it rain on one side of the street and not the other?" She looked up at Paps, who shrugged his shoulders.

"Who knows. Just one of those things." He looked down at B.J. and grinned. "I like your hat."

B.J. reached up and took his hand. "I sort of do too. Where'd you get it?"

"Wouldn't you like to know." Paps laughed. They fell into a comfortable silence again. She never did find out where the hat or rain came from, but she still had the hat and the memory.

B.J. rolled over on her side and laid the prism on the floor. A starling squawked outside, and B.J. got up to look out the window. Leaning out, she saw Put-Paws sneaking around the birdbath. Before B.J. could yell at him, Press sneaked from behind and grabbed him.

"You don't chase birds," she admonished, shaking Put-Paws angrily. She looked up to see B.J. hanging out of the window.

"What are you doing down there?" B.J. called.

"Catching Put-Paws. He was after the birds again."

"I mean, before that." Press was rarely around without some sort of plan.

"I was waiting for you. It's tadpoling time." Press propped the cat on one hip.

"I don't feel like going," replied B.J., in spite of the stirring within her.

"Well, I'm not going without you. When will you feel like it? I'm tired of playing by myself."

"You could play with Harold, or Alice, or Lollie, or even Bradley."

"Wouldn't be the same." Press sat down on the ground and tucked her cat between her legs. She mumbled something.

"What? I couldn't hear you." As B.J. leaned farther out the window, she felt the sun on her face. The warm breeze was filled with the smell of growing things.

"I said, I guess we'll have to wait."

"Why not get Alice to go?"

"Alice has decided to be a lady." Press jumped up, dropped the cat, and wiggled her hips around as she walked. She held one hand in the air and put her other hand on her hip. Press looked sideways over her shoulder. B.J. laughed, lost her balance, and almost tumbled out of the bedroom window. She caught herself on the window frame.

"Well, are we going tadpoling?" Press insisted.

"Is that all you think about? I almost fell out the window. I could be dead, you know that, don't you?"

"You could be, but you're not. Come on, let's go tadpoling. You can't hang out in your room forever. You'll get all pasty white, like a ghost. Let's go tadpoling."

B.J. felt the old familiar tugging within her. She thought it might be the call of the wild.

"Okay," she said.

CHAPTER
19

Press rode on the seat of the bicycle, carrying the Boy Scout pack on her back while B.J., standing, pedaled steadily down the old creek road. Press chattered half to herself and half to B.J., who could barely hear her over the clanky bicycle.

When they reached the old wooden foot bridge that led into the woods, B.J. brought the bicycle to a stop, jumped off, and leaned the old bicycle against one of the bridge railings. The girls crossed the bridge and made for the woods.

Squirrels chattered noisily overhead, signaling their arrival. B.J. pointed to a fallen log.

"Look over there," she whispered. Lying on its back next to the log was a baby squirrel.

"Is she dead?" Press squinted her eyes apprehensively.

"No, she's sleeping." B.J. walked in a wide circle around the log to keep from disturbing the baby squirrel. The woods were filled with chickadees and finches, feeding on the seeds of the wild flowers. Wild berries were in bloom and the floor of the woods was covered with wild violets, yellow, white, and purple.

"The berries are early this year," B.J. remarked as they passed the berry patch. "Boy, are my legs getting tired."

"Mine too."

"We're almost there. See how thick the violets are getting? We're closer to the water."

Press dropped the pack on the ground. "This pack is too heavy for me." She rubbed her shoulders.

"You learn to ride the bike and I'll carry the pack."

"I'll think about it. Where are those cans we left here last year?" Press dug around in the brush and leaves for the tin cans.

"Here's one." B.J. reached down and picked it up, brushing off the leaves and sticks. "It's rusty but I guess it'll work."

"Ah ha, here's the other one," Press said, pulling the other can out of the bushes.

"Boy, oh boy, look at that water." B.J. walked to the side of the creek bank, dropped the pack and tin cans. Press came to the creek bank and looked down, eyes wide.

"Wow! I see some," she whispered excitedly. She dropped to her stomach and hung over the water.

"Don't make a shadow, you'll scare them," B.J. cautioned, taking the tea strainer and string out of the pack. She sat down on the ground and picked up one of the tin cans. She looped the string through the holes at either side of the top and made sure that the can hung level.

Then she took the can and moved downstream from where Press was lying on her stomach. B.J. picked a spot, lay down, and lowered the tin can into the water. The can landed on its side and partially filled with water and sand. She tied the string to a tree root that stuck out of the sandy bank. Rising to her knees, she watched as the water flowed smoothly in and around the can. She rose quietly and tiptoed back to where Press was lying. "The crawdad trap is downstream," she whispered and motioned with her head. Press grunted.

"Look at that bug swimming on top of the water. He moves his back legs like arms."

They watched the water bug in silence. A frog on the opposite bank croaked loudly.

B.J. looked up just as the frog snatched a fly from the air. She watched for a moment, then turned and went back to the pack. "Let's eat," she said.

Press rolled over on her back, stretched, and yawned. B.J. unpacked the sandwiches, handed one to Press, and laid one out for herself. She dug deep into the pack for the apples her mother had given them and rolled one toward Press, who stopped it with her knee. B.J. leaned back against a tree and propped her feet on a fallen tree limb as she ate. After a while Press held up her apple core. "Think the fish will eat this?"

"No, but the squirrels will. Throw it at the bottom of that oak tree over there."

"Which is the oak tree?"

"See the one over there with the bunch of leaves up in the fork of those branches?" B.J. pointed. "That's an oak tree, and the squirrels have built a nest up in it. The squirrel will come down and eat the apple." She tried to teach Press just as Paps had taught her.

Press sat staring up at the nest, high in the tree. "How will he know that the apple is down there?"

"He'll smell it."

"From up there!"

"Sure. Remember how he chattered when he crawled underneath his nest?"

"Did he smell us then?"

"Well, not exactly. The birds warned him. They told him we were coming." B.J. tossed her apple core over next to the tree.

"Will he bite me?"

"Who?" B.J. had forgotten the squirrel and had begun digging in the pack for the cookies.

"The squirrel."

"No, silly. He isn't going to go to all the trouble of climbing down from his nest just to run over here and bite you. Why would he want to do that?"

"Maybe I smell like something good to eat."

"I doubt it." B.J. munched on a cookie. Press was fascinated that a squirrel in the top of the tree could smell so far away.

"How does he see?"

"He doesn't have to, he uses his nose. Come on, let's get going." B.J. got up and walked toward the creek.

"You mean," Press came running up behind, "that he sees with his nose?" Press wondered what it would be like to hear with your eyes or smell with your ears.

B.J. belched.

Press ran to catch up with her. "I heard that." Press laughed. "Did you do that with your mouth or your nose?"

B.J. did not turn around.

"Press, it's not nice to talk about another person's body functions."

"Body what?"

"Body functions, my body just functioned and you are not supposed to notice." B.J. stopped next to the creek bank.

"Did you know that Mr. Snelling belches with his nose?" asked Press.

"How did you know that?"

"I heard him on the playground. He didn't think anyone was around."

"What did it sound like?"

"Like this." Press belched through her nose. "Sort of like a pig snorting."

"Does it hurt?"

"No. Why don't you try it?" Press had the upper hand here and she knew it.

B.J. tossed the tea strainer into the creek. "Listen, I saw something better than that." She was not to be outdone. "Bradley Harris can blow bubbles with a straw."

"So what?" Press was unimpressed.

"So what! Well, he does it with his nose."

"Oh, that's nothing. I saw one better than that." Press tied a string on the second can for a handle, and lowered it into the water. Once the can was filled, she pulled it up and set it on the bank.

"Quick, pick it up. I've got some tadpoles in here." B.J. waved the tea strainer, Press held the can close, and B.J. turned the tea strainer over and gently slid the tadpoles into the can. She smiled. "We got some."

"I'll tie the can to this branch." Press pointed to a tree root near the bank. She finished tying the string. "I'd better check the crawdad trap." She tiptoed down the path to the crawdad trap, which lay just where B.J. had left it; lying on the sandy creek bottom, tied to a tree root. Press lay down on her stomach and peered into the can. Three crawdads were curled in the dark bottom of the can, moving lazily about in the darkness. As she watched, a crawdad shot from under a rock. The sun glistened on the surface of the water; Press could see little rings made by the swimming water bugs. She watched the water making creases along the sandy creek bottom and forgot about B.J.

B.J., in the meantime, had nearly filled the coffee can with tadpoles. She lay on her stomach and slid the tea strainer down the creek bank into the water. She watched and waited for a school of tadpoles to find her trap. Soon they appeared, moving downstream in erratic semicircles. There were tadpoles with tiny round heads and narrow sleek tails, barely visible. She scooped the strainer, catching them in midstream, and dropped them into the water-filled coffee can. She watched them swimming in quick darting motions.

As B.J. untied the string from the tea strainer, a cool breeze blew across her face. It was getting late. The breeze stirred in the trees overhead, and looking up she saw a huge mass of billowy clouds, tinged with orange, blue, and purple. In the middle was a big cloud that looked like a series of steps leading up to the sky. At the top of the cloud beams of silvery sunlight burst forth in the shape of a paper fan. After a moment the silvery streaks blended into a crystal sky and disappeared. B.J. sat studying the clouds, and thought she felt Paps nearby. It's possible, she thought, that he left by that staircase.

B.J. stood up with the tea strainer and the tadpoles just as Press came up the path carrying the crawdads. Silently the two gathered the rest of their things, then hiked back through the woods to the bicycle. B.J.

glanced back over her shoulder, and through the trees she could see the reddish-orange sun, just above where the earth met the sky. The clouds were gradually losing their shape. Suddenly she felt sure that Paps had used that stairway to wherever he went.

They rode home in silence. B.J., pedaling, thought about the clouds; Press, riding on the rear fender, concentrated on the two cans of water.

That night, as they lay on their backs in B.J.'s big double bed, fighting sleep, Press murmured drowsily, "B.J., where did you put the tadpoles?"

"Bathtub." B.J. was sinking fast. There was a long silence, followed by steady breathing.

"B.J., B.J.," Press whispered, "B.J."

"Huh?" B.J. grunted.

"How will you take a bath?" Press fought hard to stay awake.

B.J. sighed. "I won't."

Press lay quietly, smiling to herself. She rolled over and whispered, "You'll stink!" Press slowly drifted off to sleep, her head tucked close to B.J.'s arm.

"I'll take a spit bath, just like last summer," B.J. muttered, falling asleep. Press heard her just as she drifted off. She couldn't find the energy to ask what a spit bath was. She thought smelling bad might be better, though.

CHAPTER

20

The days passed quickly. Press sat on the sink, looking down into the bathtub where the tadpoles were swimming about. Their rounded bodies were getting fatter and their long narrow tails were getting shorter. Little stubby knobs were beginning to appear where their legs would be. B.J. hung over the side of the four-legged tub, and put a rock in the water. "This is for them to get up on when they get their legs." A little tadpole slithered around the rock, bumping it with his nose. He had the shortest tail and the fattest body of all. Two stubby knobs were shaping into legs, two other knobs were just beginning to form.

"What will we do when they get legs?" Press was thinking about the several bicycle trips they'd taken down the country road to haul creek water back to the tub for the tadpoles.

"We'll put them in a box and take them back to the creek." B.J. climbed up on the washstand to watch the tadpoles. Her stomach ached from her leaning over the tub. She watched the group swimming in the tub; scum was forming around the edge of the tub, making a ring.

"Won't Meg just die?" Press looked over at B.J., who was watching a tadpole skimming close to the surface of the water.

"When?"

"When she sees all that scrud in the tub."

B.J. glanced over at Press. "She won't see it, she's at Aunt Jenny's for a week. She left when Mom said we could use the tub for the tadpoles."

"I bet Meg hates spit baths." Press giggled.

"That's not the half of it. She swears she'll never take another bath."

"Will you?" Press asked.

"Sure, why not?" B.J. stood up. "You smell something?" Both girls sniffed the air.

"I smell soup," B.J. said happily. She bounded from the washstand and headed for the stairs. "And," she yelled, hitting the bottom step, "grilled cheese!"

They made a beeline for the kitchen. Martha looked up as they rounded the corner. "I thought you'd be along soon."

When they had finished the sandwiches and were drinking the last of the soup from their mugs, B.J. asked, "How much longer till the tadpoles become frogs?"

"Well, not much longer. A week or so after they get

a good start, I guess," said Martha. "I can't stand it too much longer," she added, laughing.

B.J. scratched her head. "Not much longer, then." She put her mug on the table with a thud and jumped out of the chair. "I guess we'd better find a box to take them back in." She leaned over and looked in Press's cup. She looked up at Press. "You eat slow, don't you?"

"B.J.!" Martha reprimanded. "Let Press finish her soup."

Press grinned. "It's all right, Mrs. Aiken, I'm used to it. Anyway, I'm finished. I want to go look for the box too." She hopped up. They were out the door in a flash. As they went out the back door, Press spied the crawdad can. "Boy, were those ever good crawdad tails. Wonder why Lollie and Alice wouldn't eat any?" She followed B.J. down the back steps.

"Because they're ladies, I guess," B.J. said as she pushed the bicycle to the street.

"Doesn't sound like anything I want to be," Press said, pulling herself up on the handlebar, letting her legs dangle over the front fender.

"Me either." B.J. swung her leg over the bar and kicked the pedal forward with her foot. "You still have that string in your pocket from yesterday?"

"Sure." Press gripped the handlebar tight as B.J. pedaled toward the grocery store.

"Good, we'll use it to tie the box on the back of the bicycle."

CHAPTER
21

B.J. walked gingerly around the bathtub trying to pick up the newly formed frogs. She wore her mother's rubber gloves and her jeans were rolled up to just below her knees. Press watched intently as B.J. caught one of the frogs.

"Here he comes," she yelled excitedly. Press nearly fell over from the onslaught. B.J. slid the frog into the cardboard box. The frog huddled in one corner. B.J. sat on the edge of the tub opposite Press. She wiped the beads of sweat from her face with her shirtsleeves. "Boy, this will take forever," she exclaimed.

"Will that mean past lunch *and* supper?"

"Oh, probably not." B.J. didn't want to miss two meals either. She scooped up a frog in her gloved hands. With each frog the catching got easier, until the last frog was finally collected. B.J. helped Press out of the tub, and they carried the box down the stairs.

The bicycle was leaning against the porch railing, with

B.J.'s wagon tied to its back end. They carried the box out the front door and carefully set it down on the wagon.

"You better ride on the wagon to keep the frogs from jumping out." Press looked skeptical. "I'll drive carefully," B.J. promised. She thought of the time she'd spilled Press and herself at the bottom of Wilson's hill because she'd taken the curve too fast. First Press and the wagon turned over, and then the bicycle. They ended up in Wilson's ditch. B.J. knew that Press was also remembering.

B.J. pedaled the bicycle slowly down the old dirt road, pulling Press and the frogs along behind. Press held a tin over the top of the box to keep the frogs from jumping out.

They carried the box to the side of the creek, where just weeks before they had come for the tadpoles. B.J. slid down the creek bank and stood in the cool water.

Press handed the box down to B.J., then slid down the creek bank and stood in the water next to her. B.J. set the box down on a small sandbar.

"If we let them out here, they'll find the water when they need it," B.J. observed. Paps had taught her this.

"How will they know that they need it?"

"It's just something they know." B.J. stood looking down at the box where the frogs sat motionless. Slowly she tipped the box over onto its side. Press squatted down beside her. The frogs in the box made a croaking sound. "They know they're home," B.J. said.

The two friends watched as one frog, who had moved to the side of the box, left it and hopped onto the sandbar. One by one the others followed.

ABOUT THE AUTHOR

Rae Sedgwick was born in the small rural community of Bonner Springs, Kansas. Trained as a registered nurse, she later attended the University of Iowa and the University of Kansas and earned a doctorate in psychology.

Ms. Sedgwick currently lives in her hometown of Bonner Springs, where she practices psychology and family therapy and writes a weekly column for the local newspaper. *The White Frame House* is her first novel.